Charlie

CHARLIE

Steve Powell

authorHOUSE

AuthorHouse™
1663 Liberty Drive
Bloomington, IN 47403
www.authorhouse.com
Phone: 1-800-839-8640

© 2011 by Steve Powell. All rights reserved.

No part of this book may be reproduced, stored in a retrieval system, or transmitted by any means without the written permission of the author.

First published by AuthorHouse   07/09/2011

ISBN: 978-1-4634-2478-7 (sc)
ISBN: 978-1-4634-2477-0 (dj)
ISBN: 978-1-4634-2476-3 (ebk)

Library of Congress Control Number: 2011910134

Printed in the United States of America

Any people depicted in stock imagery provided by Thinkstock are models, and such images are being used for illustrative purposes only.
Certain stock imagery © Thinkstock.

This book is printed on acid-free paper.

Because of the dynamic nature of the Internet, any web addresses or links contained in this book may have changed since publication and may no longer be valid. The views expressed in this work are solely those of the author and do not necessarily reflect the views of the publisher, and the publisher hereby disclaims any responsibility for them.

Chapter 1

November 17, 1972

"Why are you getting up so early?"
"I think there's someone at the door."
"It's too early. Who could it possibly be?"
"How would I know?"

He slipped his feet from under the warmth of the covers to the floor. While the bedroom was carpeted, the front hall was not. He looked around at his feet for yesterday's socks and pulled them on.

There was a tiny knock. This time they both heard it.

"Are you going to answer it?"

"Yes, I'm just putting my socks on."

"Oh, for Pete's sake, hurry up." She rose too. "Honestly, you are more concerned about your cold feet than anything."

"I'm going." He walked out of the room in his pajamas, turning on the hall light as he did.

She was close behind him, already in her slippers and tightening her robe. "Who could this possibly be?"

"Helen, I still don't know."

She gave him the sort of look only a spouse of fifty-some years could, a combination of frustration, love and amused affection.

As they approached the front door of their two-bedroom ranch, Ken hit the switches turning on the lights in the entry way and outside the front door. He looked out the narrow window to the right of the door, feeling Helen behind him, trying to see over his shoulder.

At first all he could see in the halos of the two lights flanking the front door was the walkway leading up to his house. The cement looked cold. He wished he had a gone to the closet and grabbed his robe.

She pushed up against him but stayed behind him. "Who is it? Can you see anyone?"

He looked on the stoop as he reached to unlock the door. Standing there in only his red plaid flannel pajamas was their next-door neighbor's oldest boy. He must have been ten by now, Ken thought. Jeez, he was barefoot. Quickly he fumbled with the lock, leaving unsaid, for once, his own frustration with his wife's need to lock and chain every door in their safe, quiet, rural home.

"It's the Williams' boy, the oldest one. Is it Michael?"

"No it's Billy, Michael is the second one. Hurry up. What is he doing here so early?"

Ken finally got the door open and he and Helen quickly pulled the boy in out of the cold, each bending to his level, instantly as worried by the boy's appearance as they were his presence this early in the morning.

They closed the door behind him and, squatting as best they could, tried to look at him eye to eye. He was obviously frightened and had been crying. The couple exchanged knowing, worried looks. They had often heard the boy's parents fighting and had discussed how difficult it must be for him and his two younger brothers.

As Helen rubbed her hands over the boy's shoulders and arms and back trying to warm him, Ken, still squatting, looked to his right, through the living room window towards the Williams' house. Through the dark woods he could see the lights were on throughout much of the house.

"What is the matter Billy? Is something wrong?" Helen asked, in a soft, kind tone that came so naturally to her.

"I can't find my Mom," he replied in an uncharacteristically small voice. Helen spent a lot of time with the Williams boys, often sitting for free when Billy's Mom, Susan, went out in the afternoons. Originally Susan had offered to pay, but Helen knew how tight money was for them and besides, she loved being with the boys, so she refused. Her casual one-time willingness to help had since evolved into a mutually agreeable free sitting service. So Helen knew Billy well and had never seen him like this.

Already Ken was hurrying back to their bedroom, pulling on a pair of khakis and his shirt and shoes. Helen grabbed a throw blanket from the living room and wrapped Billy in it, then took him into the kitchen to fix him some cocoa.

Charlie

As he grabbed his hooded parka from the front hall closet, Ken said to Helen, keeping the concern from his voice for Billy's sake, "I'll go and see what is going on. Billy, is Jim, I mean, your dad there, your brothers?"

"Mike and the baby are there. They're still asleep. I don't know where my dad is."

Ken zipped up his coat and headed out the door. Helen met him at the door and quietly said, "Be careful. You know Jim's temper."

He nodded and hurried out, genuinely concerned. Rather than going out his driveway to the road, he took the shorter way, cutting across his yard and through the woods to the Williams' house, a distance of about fifty yards. As he walked, he debated whether to go to their front door or the side door. The Williams' house was the same layout as theirs. Given the early hour and the openness of the backs of their houses, he felt that to be less intrusive, he should use the front door.

As he walked up to the house he saw that while the lights were on in the back, the front was dark. The bedrooms were in front, so he wondered if everyone was still asleep. He felt a little strange ringing the doorbell so early, potentially waking them, but given that Billy was at his house, he knew his intrusion was warranted. He pushed the bell and heard the sound of the ring that no longer worked at his own house.

Chapter 2

The dogs in the backyard started to bark. But from inside he heard nothing. He waited. Still nothing. No new lights, no sounds, nothing but the dogs.

He stood there, considering his options. While he liked Susan Williams, her husband Jim was a different story. He was one of the most aloof people Ken Bacon had ever met. Jim had served in Viet Nam and people who knew him say that when he came home he had changed. While he had always been quiet, after the war he was almost completely detached. Ken himself knew how difficult combat could be on men, having served and fought in the Pacific during World War II. But while it had affected him, seriously affected him, like most others of his generation, he tried to keep his feelings to himself. Consequently, he inwardly shook his head at men who seemed to show the impact. In Jim's case though, he felt things were different. At times he seemed angry and bitter, but Ken had trouble believing it was a result of the war.

Bacon did admire Jim's work ethic and his apparent discipline. Jim struggled to make ends meet, but it was not from a lack of trying. He was a self employed electrician and handyman and was known for doing really good work. But many of his customers felt that if his work wasn't so reliable, they wouldn't let him in their front door. He had a way of looking at people that made them feel as if they were getting a free ride.

Still, he seemed to have pretty steady work and when he wasn't out repairing things for other people, he was puttering in his own yard or fixing this or that in his own house. Additionally, when Jim became aware of how much time Helen Bacon spent watching his kids and of the fact that she wasn't charging them for it, he took it on himself to quietly try to return the favor. For example, about a year earlier, when Ken and Helen came home from a weekend in Pittsburgh visiting their son and his family, they found a neatly stacked supply of firewood in the previously depleted pile. They also saw a like-sized gap in the Williams' pile.

That was, it occurred to Bacon, the last time he had rung this doorbell. That evening Susan had answered the door. When Ken asked her about the firewood, she seemed surprised. She had invited Ken in and walked him to the family room in back of the house. She asked Jim about the wood and he had quietly said that it seemed the least he could do and wouldn't discuss it further.

Since then he had periodically found things to do for the Bacons like replacing a portion of the split rail fence in their front yard, cleaning up fallen trees or supplying them with venison and duck during hunting season. For a while after the firewood delivery, Ken had used him for handyman jobs he couldn't do himself, but he had stopped because Jim refused to accept any money for his services. Ken stopped using Jim for the same reason Jim didn't charge Ken.

And still Ken couldn't make himself like Jim and he went to great lengths to avoid having to spend time with him, despite his wife Helen's efforts.

Tentatively, he pushed the doorbell again.

Still nothing.

He walked along to the other side of the house, away from his own home and he was sure, from his wife's worried gaze. Susan's old blue Pontiac was in the driveway, but Jim's van was not in sight. As he walked further back down the driveway towards the side door, the dogs' barking became more agitated. He looked into the backyard and saw that only two of the three labs were there, tugging at their chained leads. With some sense of relief, he realized Jim wasn't there, that he must have gone hunting.

He walked up to the side door and saw that the kitchen and family room lights were all on. The family room was a large, rectangular room surrounded by windows in the very back of the house, three steps down from the kitchen. As he stepped up onto the stoop by the door, if he had chosen to look he would have been able to see most of the family room. But at this early hour he did not look inside. The dogs barked frantically. He didn't think he would even need to knock with the racket they were making. He half expected Susan to greet him, but she didn't. He slipped his left hand from the warmth of his pocket and knocked on the aluminum-held glass of the storm door. The result was a tinny-sounding, un-satisfyingly quiet knock. He doubted anyone could hear it over the sound of the dogs. He knocked again, this time on the wooden frame surrounding the door. While this knock felt more satisfying to the touch, more solid, the deeper thump seemed to dissipate in the wood. Again he doubted it could be heard over the sound of the dogs.

Reluctantly, he opened the storm door and knocked hard on the main door. This time his knock resonated. He knocked twice more, with his knuckles, trying to make himself heard. Still there was nothing but the sound of the dogs.

He stepped back and let the storm door close and then leaned over the wrought iron railing on the right side of the landing, towards the window that looked into the kitchen. He cupped his hands to the window and put his face to his hands, looking inside. There were dirty dishes on the counter and in the sink, but no sign of anyone. He knocked on the window.

Frustrated and increasingly less self-conscious and more worried, he moved to the other side of the landing and leaned to look into the window on the family room side. His eyes immediately went to an object lying on the floor at the base of the steps. He saw flesh, naked legs. It was a person. It was Susan.

His first instinct was to look away, but he couldn't. He focused, not because he wanted to, but because of what he saw. She lay there naked in a pool of blood. His eyes moved from her legs up over her torso to her head, which seemed to be the source of the blood. Through the glass he tried to make out her face, but all he saw was a mass of hair and blood and mess. All of this happened in an instant, and in that instant he realized that her skull had been bashed in. She was dead. She had to be. He knocked frantically on the window. She didn't move.

He pulled open the storm door and tried to open the main door. It was locked. He put his shoulder to the door and tried to push it open, but it didn't give at all. He pounded and, keeping his foot in the door, leaned back over the railing and looked in again, not believing what he had seen. But she was still there. He pounded frantically on the door with his right hand as he cupped the window with his left, his eyes looking at her. He never imagined he would see a sight like this again. His eyes focused, trying to make sense of her face. There was none. Eventually his intense focus left her and scanned the room. The tan carpet around her head was darkly stained and just past her above the largest stain, there was a hammer, its head covered in blood.

Chapter 3

He stepped back from the window, almost falling from the stoop. She had been murdered. He stepped back a few more steps and started to run, this time around behind the house, the short way back to his house. For the first time in years he ran, as fast as he could. As he made his way through the woods to his yard and driveway, Helen came to his own back door, opening it as she saw him running.

"What is it? What's the matter Ken?"

"Call the police, call them now." He looked for the boy. "Oh God the boy, he must have seen her. The poor kid must have seen her body before he came to our house. Could he have killed her? No." His mind raced. "No it wasn't the boy, it was his father, Jim. It must have been Jim."

He reached his own stoop and pulled Helen out, not wanting to let Billy hear what he said. "It's Susan. She's been murdered. Her body, I saw it. We have to call the police. Call from our bedroom so he doesn't hear. She's been murdered Helen, it's horrible over there."

She stared at him, stunned.

"Murdered? Is Jim there?"

"No, his van is gone and so is one of the dogs." He lowered his voice even more. "He must have done it. Oh my God, it's awful. It had to have been him."

"The other kids . . . Michael, the baby? Did you see them?"

"Oh God, the other kids. I have to go get them."

"No. We'll call the police. They'll get them."

"They might not get here for another ten or fifteen minutes. I can't let them see their mother like that, Helen. Billy must have seen her. I have to get them out of there. Call the police. Hurry, Helen, tell them there's been a murder."

He looked at her, his eyes urgent and afraid and purposeful. He raised his voice. "Call them, now."

The old man ran back to the Williams' house, again around the back. The dogs were still barking and pulling at their chains. As he ran into their yard, he picked up a rock by the edge of the driveway and ran around to the side door, pausing there. He didn't want to go in that way, didn't want to see the body again or take the boys out that way. He had to use the front door. He hurried around to the front and pulled open the storm door. The main door was locked. He tried putting his shoulder to it, but it was far too solid. He pulled his hand up into the cuff of his parka and held the rock in his protected grasp. He touched the rock to the narrow pane to the door's left, as low as he could go and still have enough window to break. He pulled the rock back and slammed it to the glass, smashing the pane. Still using the rock, he broke away the remaining shards and then reached through the opening, past his elbow. He reached inside and found the lock, turning it as he worked the knob from the outside with his right hand.

The door opened. He pulled his arm back out, cutting his parka, and hurried inside. There were no signs of violence or struggle in the front hall. As in his house, the bedrooms here were off to the right. The door to the master bedroom was open. The bed was unmade and empty. He looked around the room. Aside from the unmade bed it was neat. There were two half-filled wine glasses on the nightstand. He hurried to the next room where the kids must sleep.

The door was closed. He gathered himself and opened it, fearing the worst. His eyes went straight to bunk beds set in the back corner. The bottom bed was empty and unmade. It must have been Billy's. He looked up to the top bunk.

"Hello, um, Michael. Michael are you there?"

Under the clump of covers he saw a small movement. He hurried to the bed and stepped up onto the lower bunk's sideboard, bringing his head up above the top bunk's mattress.

"Michael, it's Mr. Bacon. It's ok. I want you to come with me, come on. It's ok."

His hand touched the blanket and he felt the boy cower. He wondered if the child was trying to hide, if he too had seen his mother. His heart sank, but still he had to hurry. He wanted to get out of there. Reaching over the boy's covered body, he pulled the whole clump back towards him.

"It's ok, Mike. I'm going to take you and the baby to our house, to Aunt Helen's. Billy is there. Come on, come with me."

Trying to hurry but not to panic the boy, Ken tucked the blanket around him and pulled him from the corner and against him and then carefully stepped down from the bunks. With now-solid footing, he shuffled the boy in his arms, making his weight more manageable and at the same time hugging him, trying to offer some comfort and reassurance.

"Where does your younger brother sleep? The baby?"

Still half asleep and very confused, the child motioned with his head, towards his parents' room. Carrying Michael, Ken hurried out into the hallway and back into the master bedroom. In the little alcove he saw the crib and couldn't believe he hadn't seen it before.

Again afraid of what he might find, he let Michael slip from his arms down onto the floor. Once the boy was standing, still wrapped in his blanket, he moved quickly across the room. The baby was there, awake and apparently fine. Ken wrapped the child in his blanket and gently lifted him from the crib. He held him in his right arm and bent to lift Michael in his stronger left. He wasn't sure if he could manage them both all the way back to his own house, but he knew he wanted to get out. As quickly as he could, he ran.

Chapter 4

As he approached his house he was surprised to hear the sound of a siren in the distance. It couldn't have been ten minutes since he had told Helen to call them. There must have been a patrol car in the area.

A few minutes later the patrol car screeched into the Williams' driveway. The car was driven by Officer David Toyne. Toyne was thirty-one and a nine year veteran of the Harrison police force. With that tenure, it was unusual for him to take the graveyard shift, but he liked to have his days free.

Toyne was driving one of the small town's two night patrol cars, his covering the more rural west side. The police department's radio dispatcher, Anne Norton, had frantically called both cars saying that there was a reported homicide at 9 Milmar Court, a small cul-de-sac off Route 161. The houses on the street were spread out with wooded, secluded lots. It was a nice street by the town's modest standards, not fancy or affluent by any means, but full of families, generally law abiding families. It was unusual for a police car to even drive down the street, let alone with its siren blaring.

After Anne had radioed the squad cars and dispatched the night shift sergeant, she called the chief, Matt Mason. Matt was up and eating breakfast when she called, at 6:42. He told her to get back on the radio and tell the patrol officers to hurry to the scene, but to talk to him before they went in. He ran to his SUV and got back on the radio and had Anne patch him through to the Bacons who had called it in.

Mason knew Ken and Helen Bacon and knew them to be level-headed. If they said there was a murder, odds are there was one. Anne patched him through and Helen answered. She explained what little she knew. The chief wished Ken hadn't gone back to the scene, but understood his motivation.

Next he tried to get Toyne on the radio. Mason tolerated Toyne. He wasn't much of a cop, but he was willing to work the night shift and in a

Charlie

small town like Harrison, that generally did not involve too much serious police work.

After several attempts Toyne finally responded. "Dave, it's Matt. Where the hell were you? I'm three minutes out. Just drive into the entrance to the driveway and tell me what you see."

"It's too late, Matt. I'm already in the driveway, next to the house. I'm gonna go in."

"No, don't. Wait. What do you see?"

"Don't go in? Why? I'm here. I have to."

Mason could hear the disappointment in his voice. "Stay by your car. I don't want you going in there without backup, without me there, Dave. I mean it. Wait. What do you see?"

Toyne was mad. He wanted to be the first in, but he also knew Mason. He knew that the chief didn't particularly like him, but that he generally did not pull rank on him.

Toyne liked the feeling of being a police officer. He liked carrying a gun and liked the respect he thought his position commanded. He also liked the night shift. With it he had a secure job that paid good money and required little work. Truthfully he spent most nights parked in some quiet spot sleeping or reading magazines, using his radar detector as a periodic alarm clock.

"I don't see anything, Chief. There is one car in the driveway; an old model beat up blue Pontiac. And there are two dogs. They're going ape-shit. Thank God they're chained up. But everything looks normal. Are we sure about this call?"

"Yeah, it came from the Bacons. I know them. Ken Bacon saw the body. I'm on 161, about two minutes out."

"Yeah, I can hear you."

As Mason pulled into Milmar Court from the north, the night shift sergeant, Kirk Weeks, was approaching from the south. He slowed and switched off his siren as he turned onto the quiet street. A few other residents were walking out to the ends of their driveways, watching and no doubt speculating as to what happened.

Mason got back on the radio. "Kirk, did you bring anyone else with you?"

"Yeah, Chief, I've got Sean O'Donnell with me."

O'Donnell was a really competent young cop with all the right instincts. Mason wished he had been the first officer on the scene and that he could go in with him initially, but it wasn't worth the hassle of sending Toyne back.

"Ok. Let Sean out at the foot of the driveway. Have him stay there and keep the neighbors back. When Paul shows up in the other patrol car, have him replace Sean and tell Sean to carefully walk up the driveway, and tell him to keep his eyes open. Everyone needs to be smart."

"Ok, Chief."

Mason pulled into the driveway, parking about ten feet behind Toyne's car. He patted his holstered handgun and zipped up his jacket. Toyne stepped from behind his car and joined Mason on the walkway to the house's side door, his pistol in hand. Mason nodded towards the drawn gun, indicating that the clearly nervous officer should keep it pointed to the ground.

"Have you seen anything?"

"Nothing Chief. Just the dogs barking, otherwise no signs of life." Toyne's voice trailed off as he finished the sentence. He instantly regretted his choice of words.

"Ok. I want you to go around back and watch the house from the corner behind us. If anyone comes out, instruct them to stop." Looking back down at Toyne's gun he said. "Don't shoot anybody."

Turning to Weeks, who was following them up the path, the chief said, "Kirk, go to the front door. Go in when you hear my signal. We don't know what we are going to find in here boys. Let's all be careful."

Mason walked up to the side door, unsnapping his holster but leaving the gun in place. There was a storm door and a solid wood door behind it, but no bell. He pulled open the storm door and knocked, calling out, "Jim? Susan? It's Matt Mason. Are you there?"

There was no response. The sun was up now and it was difficult to see in through the windows beside the door. He leaned to his left and tried to peek in, but saw only his own reflection. Reluctantly, he cupped his left hand to the glass, and, holding his right hand to his gun, brought his face to the window. This time he could see inside. He quickly scanned the room and as Ken's had earlier, his eyes immediately found the body inside.

"Holy shit."

He stepped back from the window and tried the door. It was unlocked.

He took his gun in his hand and put its point to the side of the door as he opened it. "Jim? Mr. Williams? Are you in here?"

In a louder voice so that Week's could hear him Mason shouted, "This is the police. We're coming in."

With that, he took a deep, scared breath and pushed the door open, instinctively squatting so as to not be as easy a target. His low stance put him almost immediately in front of the body. His eyes followed his extended arms and gun's point, scanning the room. Cautiously, he rose.

"Kirk?"

Weeks entered from the front, the door already wide open as he approached. On the chief's command, he had nervously entered the front hall, his boots crunching on the broken glass in the foyer. The living room was on his left and what seemed to be bedrooms were on the right. He quickly scanned the open living room, clearing it.

"Yeah, Chief, the living room's clear. There are a lot of doors up here."

"There's a body back here. Susan Williams, I think. Shit, it's a mess. This room's clear, so is the kitchen. I'm coming up your way."

As the Chief stepped from the kitchen into the hallway, following his voice, his eyes met those of his sergeant. Weeks could see that the chief was shaken. There were three doors off the hallway, two opened and one closed. Mason nodded towards the closed door, on the inside side of the hall, probably a bathroom or closet. Weeks opened it as Mason covered the hallway.

"Clear. It's a bathroom."

With his back to the inside wall, the chief made his way to the first of the two open doors. It was the boys' bedroom. He cleared that room and then the master. After they checked the closets and all of the other rooms, their anxiety lessened.

"She's back there. It's not pretty. It looks like someone took a hammer to her head."

They made their way towards the back of the house. Standing on the landing over the body on the floor beneath them, they each looked down at her.

"Fuck, Matt."

From the front door, Sean O'Donnell yelled, "You ok in there, Chief?"

"Yeah, it's all clear. Come on back."

O'Donnell made his way to the back of the house, his gun drawn too. He joined the other two officers on the landing.

"Holy Jesus."

"Yeah."

The three had the sense not to walk back down into the family room. There was no need to try to revive her or care for her. She couldn't be alive. And from the looks of her, she had been dead for some time. She lay sprawled on her side and stomach, facing the door Mason had entered. There were multiple blows to her upper torso and skull. Next to her head there was a hammer covered in blood and brain matter. The whole area around her was covered in blood, dark and to an extent congealed.

The Chief motioned for his men to stay in place. He walked down the steps, careful not to step in any of the splattered blood. He squatted and touched one of the large dollops at the outer edge of the splatter, well beyond the pool that had formed around her crushed skull. The blood was sticky but not really wet. Given the fairly large size of the spot he touched, he was surprised by how dry it felt.

"This must have happened hours ago. The killer has a big head start."

They heard footsteps on the walkway outside the still open family room door. Looking up through the windowed room, they saw Officer Toyne approaching.

He opened the storm door and looked inside, his eyes immediately drawn to the corpse.

"Oh my God, what happened? Is Jim in there too?"

"Stay out there, Dave. We don't want to walk through here. I think we're going to need some help on this one."

The chief stood back up and walked backward up into the kitchen.

"Jim's not here. We have to find him, fast. Look, we don't have the manpower to do that. He could be anywhere. Kirk, go out the front door and call the state troopers, tell them we have a murder here and that we need to find Jim Williams. Get his plates from Anne. He is a suspect, but also a spouse."

"It's pheasant season, he could be hunting. God only knows where he is."

Chapter 5

After Sergeant Weeks went to notify the state troopers, Mason turned to O'Donnell and Toyne. "Ok, you two watch the house." For emphasis he added, "From outside. I don't want anyone to touch anything. Dave, you watch the front of the house and Sean, you stand there by the side door. No one touches anything."

The chief followed his officers out of the house and closed the door behind him.

"I mean it, no one inside."

Two cruisers were blocking his car, so he decided to walk over to the Bacons'. He saw the crowd gathered out on the street and motioned for one of the other officers to follow him. The young officer, Paul Gore, hurried to catch up with the chief.

As they walked through the woods the chief pointed at the foot of the Bacons' driveway. "You stand there. No one gets by you. OK?"

"Got it, Chief."

Mason made his way to the Bacons' front door. Before he even reached the front steps, the door opened.

"Jeez Matt, what in the world happened? That poor girl."

"I don't know, Ken. I just don't know. But I need to talk to you and to the kids. How are they?"

"I don't know. They can't be good. The oldest boy, Billy, must have seen her. I don't think the second son, Mike, did. The youngest is only a baby. Come on in. They're in the family room with Helen."

The two men walked back into the kitchen. It was odd for Mason, following his friend through what was essentially the same house he had just left. Though he had been here many times before, he got sort of a nervous feeling as he walked back into kitchen and looked down into the family room.

He looked down the steps and pictured Susan's bludgeoned body there. Then he looked to the three boys sitting at the kitchen table with Helen, the baby in her arms.

In a voice that was much calmer then he felt, he said, "Hi Helen. Hi boys."

The boys were silent, their eyes downcast, both of the older ones in their pajamas. Helen had made breakfast for them, but they weren't eating. Just looking at them, he could tell they must have both seen their mother.

"Hi Matt." Helen smiled a weak smile and looked from the chief to the boys.

"Boys, you know Chief Mason. Matt, this is Billy, the oldest, he's eleven, and this is Michael, who is nine. And this is Andrew, he'll be one in February."

Both Billy and Michael looked up at the chief and respectfully smiled half smiles. Billy instinctively stood and extended his hand. Michael immediately stood too, and, mimicking his older brother, extended his little hand.

Mason stepped forward and shook Billy's hand, feeling the boy try to offer a firm grip. He smiled down at him.

"It's nice to meet you, Billy." Then he shook Michael's hand. "And you too, Michael."

In unison they responded, "It's nice to meet you too sir."

The Chief was moved by the boys' instinctive good manners, even after all that they may have seen. He had to believe that their politeness came from their mother. He wondered if that would all change now. He considered questioning them, but decided to talk to Ken first. But before he could the kitchen phone rang.

Ken tentatively answered it and then turned to him. "It's for you, Matt."

"Thanks."

He took the phone and stepped into the front hallway.

"Mason."

It was Anne, calling form the station house. "Chief, they need you back over at the Williams'."

"Ok, I'll be there in a minute. Actually, have Toyne drive one of the cruisers out on the street over here to pick me up. That way I can use the radio. Any word from state?"

"Yeah, they're on their way. And they have the APB out for Mr. Williams' van. Statewide. Does anyone know where he usually hunts?"

Charlie

"I sure don't. I think he generally goes alone. Did you tell them he might be hunting? That he had one or two dogs with him? Labs." As he said that he realized he couldn't put off questioning the boys.

"Just that he might be hunting. I'll pass along that he might have dogs with him."

Mason stretched the phone cord as far as he could, walking further up the hallway away from the boys. Lowering his voice he went on, "Ok, make it clear that he is only potentially a suspect. He is also a spouse. He should be approached cautiously, but not aggressively. Then radio Toyne. I want him to come. Have him wait for me in the driveway. Leave Weeks and O'Donnell at the crime . . . um at the Williams' house."

He hung up and walked over to the boys, sitting in an empty chair, trying to be as unimposing as he could.

He turned to the oldest boy, who, like his brother, was looking down, trying to avoid any eye contact. "Billy, was your dad home when you woke up this morning?"

"No, sir, he wasn't."

Softly, the chief added, "And your mom?"

He paused, then looking down, responded, "She wasn't home either, sir."

Mason nodded, understanding that the boy didn't want to admit seeing his mother the way he must have.

"Was he—were they home when you went to bed last night?"

"Yes, sir, they both were."

"Was anyone else there?"

"No, sir."

"Did you hear any noises last night?"

The boy's lips were trembling. His younger brother was looking into his own lap.

"Noises? No, sir."

"What time did you go to bed?"

"At nine o'clock sir. Mike went at 8:30."

"And you didn't hear anything?"

"No, sir."

"No voices? No dogs barking? Cars?"

"No, sir, nothing."

Mason knew he had heard more. The poor kid was in agony. But he also knew that he was not the right person to try to get the information from him. The boy and his brother had already been through enough.

He turned to Michael. "How about you, Mike? Did you hear anything?"

In a barely audible voice he responded, "No, sir."

"Ok. And your mom and dad were both home when you went to bed?"

"Yes, Sir. Dad read to us and said our prayers, then Mom came in and kissed us goodnight."

"Your dad read to you? To both of you?"

"Yes, Sir," Mike answered. "Dad reads to us every night and then at 8:30 I have to turn my light off. Billy gets to read till nine."

"Did someone come in at nine to tell you to turn out your light?"

"Yes sir. Dad."

"Ok, thanks, boys." He stood up, patting Billy on the shoulder. As he stepped away from the table, he turned back and asked, "What was your dad reading to you?"

They both responded, "*The Yearling*." Mike added, "We're almost done."

"Thanks, boys." The chief smiled at them and Helen.

"Helen, would you mind watching the boys for a while?"

"Of course not, Matt."

With his right hand, he touched Ken's elbow and nodded to him to follow him from the kitchen. They walked through the hallway to living room, again as far from the boys as they could get.

"So what happened, Ken?"

Bacon recounted the morning from the initial knock to his two trips to the Williams' house.

"Do you know the Williams well? From the sound of it, you spend a lot of time with them."

"Well, I don't. Helen does. She watches the kids for Susan for a couple hours most weekdays. Well, just the baby now that the boys are back in school. And then all three if they get home from school before Susan gets home."

They heard a car pull into the driveway and looked up to see officer Toyne pull in. Mason regretted asking for Toyne.

"Ok, thanks, Ken." He gripped his friend's shoulder, looking him straight in the eye. "You did well. Really you did. I'm going to have Sean O'Donnell come back over here and take your statement. I want you to try to remember

Charlie

everything you can. Give him as much detail as you can. Anything and everything you can remember, okay?"

"Sure, of course."

"Do you think Helen would mind watching the kids for a while longer, until we can find some family? I asked her, but after all that has happened, I want to be sure you're okay with it."

"Sure, like I said, she watches them most days anyways. She is Aunt Helen to them."

"Really? Aunt Helen? I didn't know that."

"Yeah, she has been watching them for over a year now."

The chief shook his friend's hand and started to leave.

"Listen, Ken. Don't ask the kids any questions about last night or this morning. Try to remember anything they say, but don't question them. The poor kids must have seen her, at least the oldest one. We'll get someone from the state to question them. Someone who knows how to ask."

"I understand. Billy must have seen her, but I don't think Mike did. But either way, we are just going to try to comfort them as best we can."

Chapter 6

Toyne drove the chief back to the Williams' driveway and found most of the neighbors standing there. There were also two state trooper's cruisers parked at the end of the now-crowded driveway. Toyne parked out on the street behind them. As they stepped from the car the neighbors shouted out questions.

"Folks, please just stand back, there is nothing to see here. We have police business to conduct, please give us room to do it."

Quietly to Toyne he added, "Listen, I want you to question everyone here, try to do it one on one. Just see if they heard anything here last night or if they noticed anyone coming or going last night or this morning. If they heard or saw anything at all, you know the routine."

"Ok, Chief. Are you sure you don't want me in the house?"

"Yeah, Dave, we need these statements."

"OK."

He could tell Toyne was mad, but he didn't care. Immediately he went to the state troopers. They were arguing with Sergeant Weeks about getting in the house.

"Hi men, I'm Chief Mason. I told Sergeant Weeks to keep everyone out until I got back." To diffuse their anger he added, "Listen, there is a murder in there and I don't want anyone to go in there until the forensics guys have gone through it. One of my officers, Sergeant Weeks and I cleared the house earlier. The victim is the only one left in there."

The officers couldn't disagree with his thought process and one went to his car to check on the status of the hunt for Jim Williams and his van.

Chapter 7

Three hours later there was still no sign of Williams or his van. Local police departments all over western Pennsylvania, New York, eastern Ohio and northern West Virginia had been notified and were, in addition to checking highways and rural routes, searching hunting areas for his van.

At 11:45, the local police department in Concord, Pennsylvania, a very rural area in the northwestern part of the state, found it.

The officer who found the van was Dan Kipp. Kipp, a bit of a hunter himself, had been checking various spots in the area that he knew other hunters used to park for day or weekend hunting trips. He found the van at the end of a very long dirt road, not the sort of spot one happened upon. In his mind, the driver of the van had to have been here before.

Kipp radioed in his finding and then approached the closed-paneled van with his gun drawn. He called out nervously, but from the looks of it, even from a distance, thought it was empty. From about twenty yards out, he made a broad circle around to the front of the van, calling out all along. Cautiously he approached from the front and then from the passenger side. There was no one inside. However, he did see two empty shell boxes sitting on the passenger seat. While he might only be hunting, the man they were searching for was armed.

In the dirt around the truck, there were fresh boot and dog tracks. The tracks, especially the dog tracks, were random, but eventually headed off to the northeast, into the woods.

Kipp went back to his car and radioed in his findings, suggesting that someone call the state police and have them bring in their dogs. With the dogs, he felt Williams should be pretty easy to find.

The officer sat in his car, contemplating waiting for the state troopers. But after about five minutes he got antsy, and decided to go off on his own.

At first the tracks left by the man and his dog were pretty easy to follow. They led up over a ridge and then back down the other side. Williams was not following any path, but rather cutting his own way. What made Kipp's task easier was that Williams seemed to be heading in a pretty straight direction, still to the northeast. After about twenty minutes he followed the tracks into a scrub covered clearing. From there the tracking grew more difficult. His first tactic was to try to find and follow tracks. Unfortunately the scrub was too short and the cover too thick for Williams or his dog to leave any obvious tracks.

When that failed he moved back to the entrance to the clearing and then tried following the straight path Williams had been following. He walked about ten yards back in to the woods and then turned and followed his path back to the clearing. Along that line he picked a spruce at the other side of the clearing and using it as a marker, walked towards it. The clearing itself was almost a half a mile across, so it seemed unlikely that Williams would be following as straight a path as he was, especially if he was letting his dog lead, as he might have done before he started hunting in earnest, if he was, in fact, hunting at all.

Seven or eight minutes later he reached the spruce or at least the line of the spruce. The tree itself was set back from the clearing. He walked about fifteen yards into the woods, where the ground cover became sparse, and started his search for tracks. There were none right there, so he took note of the trees where he started. Looking into the woods on either side of him he thought better of that and scuffed up the dirt under his feet and then gathered some sticks and built up a little teepee shaped pile, to better mark his starting and entry point. He also made note of the time, 12:25. Walking first to the east, parallel to the edge of the clearing, he made the straightest path he could, fifteen yards in from the clearing, looking for tracks. He went in that general direction for about ten minutes, finding nothing.

Disheartened, he turned around and made his way back. After five minutes his focus shifted from looking solely for tracks to looking for his pile of sticks. He started to wish he had left his hat or jacket perched at the edge of the clearing, but had decided against doing that because if he did find William's trail, he did not want to have to double back to find his Hansel and Gretel belongings. He imagined the shit his pals would give him if rather than finding the suspect or victim's husband, he himself got lost. Then he wondered if while he was wondering about getting lost, he had missed his stick pile.

As his self doubt grew and grew, he considered turning back again. He looked at his watch, 12:43. He decided to keep going forward until 12:47, maybe 12:48. He conscientiously kept his gaze about five or ten feet in front of him, panning from left to right, looking more for his stick pile than for tracks. About a minute later he found it. To play things safe he gathered more sticks and made a second pile. Satisfied that he would be able to find his entry point again, he ventured to the west. Once again he tried to pan an area of about ten feet as he walked. This time, after about three minutes, he found dog tracks and boot tracks as well. They led north. Again he followed them, and again it was clear Williams was generally going in a fairly straight direction, which made Kipp's job easier. After about twenty minutes however, he lost all track of them. He decided to just keep going forward, heading north.

"Officer."

Kipp literally jumped when he heard the voice. He looked off to his left and saw a man squatting, a shotgun in his hands, across his lap pointing to the ground and away from Kipp. The man was slender and wiry, the thin skin of his face wrinkled around his eyes. He looked older than forty-one, the age reported on the APB, but with the lab sitting silently, obediently behind him, there was little doubt it was Williams. His face gave away nothing, neither amusement at having startled him nor any regret for having done so. Kipp sized him up as tough, very tough.

"Mr. Williams?"

Williams face registered genuine surprise when the policeman called him by name, surprise that quickly changed to concern.

"Yes. What happened?" Williams stood and stepped towards him. The dog stayed in place. Kipp instinctively moved his right hand to his side, touching his holstered handgun. Seeing his action Williams stopped, the look on his face changing. He looked to his left and right, then seeing a large tree immediately to his left, stepped to it and rested his shotgun there, its butt to the ground. He stepped back away from the gun and repeated his question. "What is going on, Officer?"

Kipp watched. He was reassured by the man's actions, but was not ready to let his guard down. So far everything Williams had done seemed to suggest that he did not suspect that he was being pursued by the police. Kipp considered his options. They were at least forty minutes from their cars and another couple of hours from Williams' hometown. Kipp did not know if it would be fair to leave the man wondering what was the matter for that long. But likewise, he did not want to tell a potential murderer that he was on to him. Still if he was the murderer, he would know anyway, and it seems unlikely he would have been so surprised when Kipp knew his name, nor would he have so easily given up his gun. Kipp looked at the shotgun again.

"What has happened?" Williams look was of concern and some anger now, too.

"All I know, Mr. Williams, is that officers are looking for you all over the state."

"That's all you were told?" Williams moved towards his gun. As he did Kipp tensed. He stopped.

"Look, what's going on? If it makes you more comfortable, you take the gun." Williams moved further away, leaving a wide gap between him and the shotgun. Kipp stepped to it and picked it up. It was a twelve gauge Remington. The safety was on.

"Mr. Williams, there has been some sort of an incident at your home. That is all I know, sir."

Williams shouted to the dog. "Come."

The lab quickly came to him and they started heading back in the direction from which they had both come. Kipp fell in behind, grateful to follow, both to keep his eye on Williams and to let him lead, as he seemed quite sure of the route.

"Tell me specifically what you were told, Officer."

"Kipp, Dan Kipp. Like I said, Mr. Williams, all I know is that there is an APB out for you, for your van and you. We were to find you, and get you home, sir. Not to arrest you, but to bring you to your home." He did not add that he was told that Williams was potentially a suspect in a homicide and that he was to approach with caution.

Williams looked back at him, clearly not believing that he was getting the whole story, but not pressing either. Frustrated, he increased the pace. Kipp struggled to keep up. Eventually they came to the clearing. In the distance they could both hear a chopper.

"Is that for us?"

Williams didn't wait for Kipp to respond, instead he hurried out into the clearing and the second he reached it, he looked in the direction the sound of the chopper was coming from. They couldn't see it anywhere. Williams led Kipp to the middle of the field. After a moment or two the helicopter sounded as though it was coming closer. Williams started to wave his hands over his head, trying to attract its attention.

Kipp stayed back a bit, watching both the chopper and Williams.

The chopper saw him and turned towards them.

"Is he going to pick us up?"

"I don't think so, Mr. Williams. He was probably just part of the team trying to find you."

The chopper hovered about three hundred feet over them, trying to survey the situation.

Kipp waved up to the pilot and gave him an okay signal.

Williams yelled to him, "If he's not going to pick us up, let's stop wasting time." And with that he started off again, towards the other side of the clearing.

As he followed, Kipp studied the man in front of him. Everything he had done so far suggested that he was innocent and unaware of what was going on. All Williams knew was that something was wrong at home and that the authorities were concerned enough to send out a group to find him, a group that included a helicopter. Kipp had trouble believing that this man had killed his wife.

For the next fifteen minutes, the two men and the dog made their way back to their vehicles. When they got close, Kipp and Williams were surprised to see a group of state troopers and Concord officers heading towards them, several with their guns drawn.

To calm the situation, Kipp said to Williams, "Step behind me and call the dog back, too."

Williams nodded and stopped and Kipp stood in front of him and to his left so that the approaching officers could clearly see Williams, and so that Kipp could be sort of a buffer. The officers started to spread out.

Kipp addressed the two officers from the Concord Police Department, trying to quickly diffuse what was becoming a tense situation. "Everything is okay, guys. This is Mr. Williams. Mr. Williams, this is Greg Henderson and Bill Cochran, from the department where I work."

Seeing how Kipp was trying to put everyone at ease, Williams stepped forward and extended his hand to the officers.

The adrenalin-pumped officers were disarmed by the pair's actions. The chopper had radioed in that Kipp and Williams were heading back towards their vehicles, about twenty minutes out and that they seemed to be doing so without any sign of tension or duress. While that had tempered the officers' blood lust to an extent, they had still initially approached as if they were part of a manhunt, circling in on a potential killer.

Henderson and Cochran extended their hands warily, but were reassured as Kipp smiled and nodded from behind Williams. To further ease the tension, Kipp stepped to the state troopers, his back to Williams and introduced himself.

"What has happened? What is going on at my house?"

Henderson shook Williams' hand and responded, "I'm not exactly sure, sir. I was only told that Officer Kipp found your car and that there has been an incident at your house. We are to escort you back to Harrison as quickly as possible.

One of the trooper's stepped forward. "Mr. Williams, I'm Lieutenant Norm Armour, from the Pennsylvania State Police. I'm afraid I have some very bad news, sir."

The other four officers stepped closer, all anxiously watching Williams.

"Officer, what is this all about?"

The trooper looked from Williams to Kipp. Kipp shook his head.

"Sir, it's your wife."

Williams stepped towards him. "What? What has happened?"

The officer hesitated then said, "She's dead, sir. She's been murdered."

All five men watched William's reaction carefully. His face registered very little. He just stood there, looking the officer in the eye. Then he turned to Kipp.

"What happened? Are my boys alright?"

Kipp looked at him, and responded, "I really don't know, Mr. Williams."

The trooper put his hand on William's shoulder, not in a friendly or a menacing way, but with some authority. "Your children are fine, sir. I believe they are with a neighbor. Come with us. We'll get you back."

"What happened to my wife? She was murdered? Who?"

"Honestly, Mr. Williams, I've told you everything I know."

The second trooper stayed back for a moment, keeping a distance between Williams and his colleague, watching Williams' every movement. As he watched, he quietly said to Kipp, "Did you frisk him?"

Kipp responded, a little embarrassed, "No. When I came upon him he surrendered his shotgun." He extended his hands. "This is it. He gave it to me without my asking, when he saw that I was concerned about him holding it."

The trooper looked at Kipp then approached Williams. "Mr. Williams, are you carrying any other weapons?"

Williams was standing in apparent shock by the news of his wife. He didn't seem to have heard the trooper's question.

The trooper asked again, "Mr. Williams?"

Williams turned to him and looked up, his face blank, his eyes unfocused. "I'm sorry, what?"

The trooper repeated himself, this time a little softer. "Are you carrying any other weapons, sir?"

His eyes came into focus and the words slowly registered, as well as their implication. "No . . . well yes."

He opened his jacket and revealed the sheathed hunting knife on his belt. He pointed toward it and nodded and the officer nodded in response. Williams unfastened his belt and slipped the sheath from it and handed it by the handle to the officer.

"I also have shells in this pocket." He pointed to the left pocket of his hunting jacket.

The officer stepped forward and reached into the pocket while the others carefully watched, Lieutenant Armour with his hand on his holstered sidearm. After he removed the shotgun shells, the officer carefully frisked him.

Williams stood still as he was searched, looking at the men around him. Only Kipp seemed at ease.

Satisfied that there were no other weapons, the trooper stepped back and nodded to the Lieutenant.

"Okay, let's get back to the parking area."

Chapter 3

Ten minutes later they were back at the cars. There were two other troopers there and a total of five vehicles.

Kipp said to the troopers, "I am going to drive Mr. Williams down to Harrison."

The Lieutenant responded, "No. We'll take care of that, officer."

Knowing he had no authority over the troopers, he responded, "Well at the very least I'd like to ride down with you guys."

"What about my van?"

Armour responded. "We'll take care of that for now, sir."

Without any hesitation Williams reached into his coat pocket and handed Armour the keys. The significance of his action wasn't lost on anyone except Williams himself.

Williams said, "Let's go. Which car."

The Lieutenant pointed to his state vehicle.

Williams snapped his finger and his lab started to follow him to the car.

"Sir, we'll get the dog down to you later." Looking at the two policemen from the Concord PD, he added, "These officers will watch him. He'll be fine, sir."

Chapter 9

Jerry Miller was the prosecutor for Kramer County, Pennsylvania. He had just been re-elected so while he was not facing the pressures of a pending election, a murder in his quiet part of the state was not something voters tolerated under any circumstances. He had to find, try and convict the murderer and from his thirty plus years of experience, he knew that if he was going to do that, he had to get on top of things fast.

He was first notified of the murder by phone at about 7:30 that morning. Matt Mason's office had notified the DA's office after they had called the state troopers to try to find the victim's husband, who was at this point, primary suspect in the murder.

When the husband's van had been found, at 11:45, a full five hours had passed since the victim's son had knocked on the neighbor's door and probably eight to twelve had passed since the actual murder. In that time, the husband, Jim Williams, could have easily driven from Harrison up to Concord. With traffic the drive would take about three hours. In the early morning, it would take about two and half. So the husband did not yet have a clear alibi.

The DA had arrived at the murder scene, the victim's house, at about 8:00 that morning. Over the years Miller had seen a lot of bodies, but this one was really bad. To make matters worse, it was probable that at least one of the victim's children, a young boy, must have seen his mother's bludgeoned body. Miller, who had children of his own, couldn't imagine how they could ever get over seeing something like that. He immediately delegated the task of finding the boys' nearest relatives to his longtime assistant, Ann Haggerty.

The DA focused on the facts themselves. He was briefed by Chief Mason, whom Miller had always found to be very competent if not somewhat old fashioned. From what had been pieced together so far, when the children had gone to bed the night before, both their mother and father had been home. The police had been called at 6:40 and arrived on the scene at 6:49, just nine minutes later. A squad car had been in the area. The police found the house open, the side door unlocked and the front door left wide open by a neighbor, a Ken Bacon. Mason explained that Bacon had broken a windowpane and reached in to unlock the front door, presumably to avoid having to confront the body, which was just inside the side door.

When he briefed Miller, Mason said they had only gotten a preliminary statement from Bacon. When they got a full statement, which would be one of the next things Mason and his men did, the chief said he would press Bacon on why he didn't entered through the side door, first to check to make sure she was in fact dead, and on his second visit, to avoid having to break in.

Beyond that, they had the murder weapon, a hammer, most likely Williams' hammer. At this point they had not established whose prints, if any, were on the handle. It seemed clear that the murder took place where the body was found and there did not appear to be any sign of forced entry, other than Bacon's, before the murder. Bacon's alibi was, for whatever it was worth, his wife. However, Mason explained that Bacon was an unlikely suspect. The man was in his early seventies and was a good friend of the chief's. It seemed very unlikely that he was anything other than a good neighbor.

At the time of his initial briefing, Williams hadn't yet been found. Aside from the body and the murder weapon, the officers on the scene hadn't discovered much else. The children, the Bacons, the evidence at the crime scene and any evidence they might find in Williams' van or on his person were all they had to go on. At this point, all that Miller could do was to wait. The coroner had arrived and was examining the body and the scene along with some specialists from the state police.

Chapter 10

After he finished briefing Miller, Mason walked back over to Ken Bacon's house. The crowd of neighbors and reporters out on the street was growing, but they were at least on the far side of the road, kept there at bay by two of his men and an increasing number of state troopers and their vehicles. He could see Officer Toyne standing away from the group with another man, a civilian, apparently taking his statement.

As he approached the Bacon's house, coming through the woods to avoid the neighbors and the gathering press, he was surprised to see more state troopers standing in the driveway, mostly just talking with each other. He nodded to them and walked up the front steps. Feeling somewhat self-conscious, he knocked on the front door and at the same time opened it. To his left he saw O'Donnell talking with Helen Bacon. Both rose as he stepped into the foyer.

"Hi, Chief. I'm just finishing up on Mrs. Bacon's statement. Mr. Bacon is in back with the kids . . . well, except for the baby. He's sleeping in there." O'Donnell pointed to the master bedroom.

"Great, Sean. Thanks." He turned his attention to Helen. "How are the boys doing? Have they said anything?"

"Nothing, Matt. The poor things. I don't know what to do." She lowered her voice. "Have you been able to find Jim? Did he, well, did he do it?"

"No, we haven't found him yet, Helen, and I have no idea who did it. Do you think he is capable of something like that? You spent a lot of time over there. Were there fights? Were they happy?"

She looked at him, surprised to hear him asking her questions, especially such personal questions. In all the years she had known Matt and his wife, Helen could not ever remember him asking a prying question about anyone else. He was as circumspect and uninterested in such things as her own husband. Seeing him in this questioning mode sort of threw her.

He saw the confusion on her face and tried to settle her. He reached out and touched her shoulder. "You and Ken have done everything just right, Helen. But you know these people well. I need to gather every bit of information I can about them to figure out why this happened. Do you think Jim is capable of killing someone, of killing his wife?"

She looked at him and considered it for a moment. She knew her husband had killed during the war and knew the impact it still had on him all these years later. She also knew that Jim had served in Viet Nam and that he had seen combat there. She had no doubt that he had killed there and suspected that he had probably been good at it. She didn't think, as she thought about it, didn't think that he would have enjoyed it, but she had no doubt that he was capable of it and in fact probably had been a very good soldier. He certainly came home with a lot of medals.

She lowered her voice again. "I think he could kill, yes. And I know that he and Susan were having problems, mostly financial problems, but we could hear them fight. He was . . . he is a very difficult man, a very unhappy man, Matt."

"Ok. Thanks, Helen. There will be lots more questions. In fact one I need to ask right now. Does she have any relatives around here? Siblings? Her parents?"

"No siblings, most of her family is around Philadelphia. Her parents live there. I have their number somewhere."

"Great, could you please find it for me?"

She nodded and awkwardly left the room. Mason turned to O'Donnell. "Did you get anything surprising from them?"

"Yes, Chief. One really surprising thing from Mr. Bacon. He said when he first went over there, when he was trying to find the boys' parents and found the body . . . he said that when he saw her body there that he tried to open the back door and that it was locked. He said he even put his shoulder to it. Remember when you went in? It was unlocked, wasn't it? He only just told me, I was on my way over to let you know, Chief."

The Chief looked at him in shock. The implication was that the murderer must have been in the house when Bacon first came over.

"Did you tell Mr. Bacon that we found the door unlocked?"

"No, Chief, of course not. I pressed him on it, to be sure he was certain, but I didn't give away any information. But Bacon said Williams' van was not in the driveway when he first got there. So either Mr. Williams had hidden the van or someone else killed her and whoever that was approached the house by foot."

The Chief looked at his watch. It was 9:50 AM. Bacon left the house the first time at about 6:30 AM and the second time at about 6:45 AM. If the killer left between his trips or after the second trip, then he couldn't have been on the road for more than about three hours.

Mason went back out front. He talked with the state troopers and explained, without divulging details, that the killer had probably not left the crime scene any time before between 6:30 and 6:45 AM and no later than 6:50 when the first policeman arrived on the scene.

They had to find Jim Williams to establish whether he could have been there. The troopers got on the radio and spread that news, refining the search area to a range of no greater than about two hundred to two hundred and fifty miles around Harrison.

Chapter 11

A couple of hours later the chief received news that Williams had been found up near Concord in the northwestern part of the state. He was on his way back to Harrison, driven by some state troopers.

Two and a half hours after that, as the troopers' cruiser reached Harrison, the police viewed him as their primary suspect. When the cruiser pulled into his small rural street, Williams was surprised to see at least a dozen marked and unmarked police cars, and near the foot of his driveway, a gathering of his neighbors.

He stepped from the police car and made his way down the street towards his driveway and the crowd. When his neighbors saw him they all became quiet, watching him, but avoiding his eyes. While he had never been close to any of them, he had always been willing to help them with broken appliances, leaks or other small problems. He rarely charged any of them for smaller jobs; he simply had helped.

Now, while he felt a sense of sympathy from some, and even a soft touch or two on his back as he passed through, he got a different sense from others. As he squeezed by, one mother took her young son by the shoulders and pulled him back, shielding him from Williams. She seemed both afraid and angry.

Once passed the quiet crowd, he stepped around the police car that blocked the entrance to his driveway. As he did he heard David Toyne, an officer he vaguely knew, saying into his car radio, "He's here, Chief, walking down his driveway. Okay, yes, yes."

"Mr. Williams. Mr. Williams, stop."

Williams stopped and faced him.

"Chief Mason wants you to go next door, to the Bacons'. Your boys are over there."

"But my wife, I want to see my wife."

Charlie

The nearby crowd was silent, listening to every word.

Toyne looked back at the crowd and then to Williams. "You don't want to go back there."

Williams had had enough. For hours now his questions had been ignored. He started down his driveway towards his house.

Toyne tried to sound more authoritative.

"Mr. Williams, stop. Stop!"

Williams didn't stop. He increased his pace. About half way down his driveway three state troopers who were standing there saw him approaching and saw the local officer hurrying after him. Instinctively they stepped in front of him.

"Let me by. This is my house."

"Stop him."

Williams moved to go around the troopers, not slowing his pace.

"Sir, you can't go back there. It's a crime scene." The trooper stepped in front of him holding up his hands, one of which held a Styrofoam cup of coffee.

Williams kept going. The officer jumped back to avoid spilling the coffee and slammed into the trooper behind him. As a result, he both spilled his coffee all over his arm and caused the trooper behind him to stumble. The first trooper threw his cup to the ground and the second, startled by the sudden action, jumped around the first and grabbed Williams by the shoulder.

Williams shook him off and started to run towards his house. The officers, confused and not used to being ignored, took off after him. Two other troopers standing beside the driveway right in front of the house saw Williams now running towards them and the other troopers chasing him. They too stepped out in front of Williams and formed a makeshift wall stretching out their arms. Williams put his head down and tried to blow right through.

The two slowed him and as the three from behind caught up, they all grabbed at him. Williams struggled and the trooper who had been bumped into threw a punch, hitting Williams on the back of his head, on his upper neck. The blow knocked Williams forward and his forehead slammed into the face of one of the troopers who was blocking him, smashing the officer's nose. Blood gushed from the officer's face. When the other troopers saw the blood, they instantly became more aggressive. Even as Williams fell forward the troopers started to pummel him. In an instant he was on the ground, with four of the state troopers on him, two still punching him.

With all of the policemen on the driveway now on top of Williams, the crowd at the end of the driveway made its way towards the house and Williams and the officers . . . towards the brawl. Three of the officers were kneeling on him and another was struggling to cuff him. The fifth officer stood with his hands on his face, blood streaming down.

After he was finally held and cuffed, the officers roughly lifted Williams to his feet. His face was also bleeding and he continued to struggle, trying to make his way to the house. Even cuffed, he was hard to hold. He raised a knee into the officer in front of him and with that a second brawl started. This time three of the officers simply unleashed on him, punching and kicking him until he was back on the ground. The neighbors, now about fifteen feet from the rumble, stood silently, shocked by the violent scene.

From the woods they saw their own police chief come running. To their surprise, he started to yell at the troopers. "What in the Sam Hell are you idiots doing?"

Still on top of Williams, the troopers looked up, rage in their eyes. Chief Mason pushed the troopers off of Williams and helped him to his feet.

"What is the matter with you guys?" He took the cuffed Williams by the arm and pulled him up and away from the officers and his house. As he did he saw the neighbors there and saw the looks of horror on their faces.

He turned to his own officers and said, "Get these people off this property now! What are they doing here, what the hell happened? Get them back and I mean now!"

The neighbors, many of whom knew Chief Mason, had never seen him so angry. Before the officers could even react to the chief's complete authority, the crowd did, turning and hurrying down the driveway.

Mason led Williams to the side, away from the neighbors, the still-angry state troopers and the house onto his front lawn. He moved behind Williams, his hands gently but firmly holding his shoulders.

"I'm sorry Jim. This shouldn't have happened." Still holding one of Williams' shoulders, the chief fumbled to find his keys and then started to uncuff him.

"I'm going to uncuff you. I want you to stay calm, Jim. You can't go back to the house right now." He paused and then added, "You don't want to go back there."

As Mason uncuffed him, Williams turned to face him. "What happened? Where is Susan? Where are my children."

"The boys are fine. They're next door at the Bacons'."

"Where is Susan? What is going on?"

Williams looked Mason straight in the eye.

"She's dead, Jim. She's been murdered, bludgeoned to death."

Mason watched his reaction carefully. At first he saw shock, genuine shock in the man's eyes, but after a moment they turned cold.

"Bludgeoned? How? Who? What happened?"

He started toward the house again. Chief Mason took his arm.

"Jim, you can't go back there."

Williams looked from the house back to the chief.

"What happened? Who did it? Are the boys alright?"

"The boys are fine. They weren't touched, at least so far as I can tell. I've spoken with Billy. He went over to the Bacon's and got them this morning."

Mason watched as Williams processed all of this.

"He went over to the Bacons'?"

"He must have seen her body, Jim. He says he didn't, but he must have. At a little after six this morning he went over and knocked on their door, said he couldn't find his mom."

Mason stopped himself, torn between wanting to tell a father about a horrible scene his son must have seen and fulfilling his role as a police chief, questioning a potential suspect.

He watched Williams. He had always known him to be a guarded man, slow to show any emotion, good or bad. People took that reserve as coldness, but Mason had never thought that to be the case. Truth be told, he had always sort of liked the way Williams carried himself. He was a hardworking, quiet man. Word was that he had seen some horrible things in Viet Nam and had handled himself extremely well there, but those stories had never come from Williams himself.

Mason had trouble believing that Williams could have done what had been done back in the house to his wife. He had seemed genuinely shocked when he heard the news of how she was murdered and still did.

"Who did it?"

"We don't know, Jim."

"How was she killed?"

The Chief looked around. The troopers and even his own men were staring menacingly their way. He had to get control of the interview. Regardless of what his gut told him, Williams was the prime suspect and the chief's job was to get information from him, not to give it to him.

"Come on, let's go sit in my car. There are too many people around here. I have to ask you some questions and then I'll take you to see your boys."

Williams started to resist, but he seemed to understand and resigned himself to answering the Chief's questions.

Rather than walking out the driveway, the Chief led Williams through the woods out to the street. He waved to one of his men to join them.

"Bill, I'm going to use your car to talk with Mr. Williams. There are too many people around my truck. I want you to stay on the road and keep everyone clear of us. No civilians and no troopers. Just keep everyone back."

The officer hurried on ahead and as they walked the chief started his questioning.

"When did you last see your wife?"

"Yesterday. I got home from work, did a few chores, had dinner with Susan and the boys and then after the boys went to bed, I packed up my hunting gear and left, at around 9:45. Maybe 10:00."

"Did anyone see you leave?"

"I don't know."

"Did you buy gas last night, make any stops on the way to Concord?"

Williams noted that the chief already knew where he had been. His eyes registered understanding. He realized he was a suspect. He paused for a moment and then responded.

"No, I gassed up yesterday morning, at Phil's in town. Last night I did stop once, to let the dog go to the bathroom, but it was just at a quiet spot on the road. I don't know if anyone saw me."

"Where did you sleep last night?"

"Up in, well outside of Concord, near where I parked my truck. It was clear. I didn't even need to pitch my tent. I just set out my ground sheet and slept in my sleeping bag."

"Why did you go all the way up there?"

"I lived up there for a while as a kid, learned to hunt and fish there. It's a great area, much better hunting than around here."

"What time did you get up?"

"Around five, before sun up. Had some coffee from the thermos, fed the dog and headed off. Didn't see anyone until the policeman from Concord found me, or I should say until I found him."

No alibi the chief thought. He could have killed her, gone up to the woods, buried his clothes and never been seen by anyone.

"Jim, I have some tough personal questions I have to ask, so you might as well just answer them."

He looked at Williams squarely. Williams held his gaze.

"How were things between you and Susan?"

"Fine."

"Really?"

"Yes, fine."

"Did you fight with her last night?"

Mason watched as Williams thought about his question. His face revealed nothing.

"Yeah, we argued."

"About what?"

"About the things husbands and wives always argue about. You can't think I did this."

The chief pressed. "About what Jim?"

Williams looked at him, a proud man, a man not used to discussing much of anything with anyone outside his family, let alone personal matters.

"We fought about money."

"Did you hit her?"

"No, of course not. We argued. Out in our backyard. I guess the neighbors heard us."

"And how did you resolve the argument?"

"We didn't. Money's tight. Money's always tight. All the arguing in the world isn't going to change that."

"Did you hit her?"

"No. Look, Mason, I've answered your questions, now tell me what happened."

The chief looked at him and then said. "You only took one dog hunting with you, is that right?"

"Yeah, generally I take one and leave two at home. Last night I took Brandy and left the other two."

"Yeah, so I noticed. They have been barking all morning. They seem like pretty good watchdogs. Ken Bacon said they were barking like crazy when he approached this morning. But he didn't hear them much last night. Susan was murdered in the back of the house Jim, in the family room. There was apparently quite a struggle. It's hard to believe the dogs wouldn't have barked a lot when a stranger approached the house, let alone when the struggle happened. The windows of the family room were open. How do you explain them not barking?"

"I don't know."

"Every time an officer walks down that driveway, they bark. You can hear them now. How do you explain them not barking last night?"

"I don't know. You said there was quite a struggle. What happened, tell me? What happened to my wife?"

Mason looked at him again and then down to the dashboard. He thought for a moment then looked back up at Williams. "She was bludgeoned to death, with a hammer. With your hammer."

Williams stood listening. He sometimes worked construction and he engraved his initials on all of his tools. He realized that must be how the chief knew it was his hammer.

"There was a struggle?"

"Yes."

"Is she still back there?"

"Yes. The coroner from Stamford got here about an hour or two ago. He has to clear the scene. Plus there are some specialists from the state police who just got here. They are also going over the scene. I'm sure they will all want to question you."

"Billy walked over to the Bacons'? He said he couldn't find her?"

Mason just nodded.

"Was she hidden, covered up?"

Mason didn't know what to do. He couldn't give the prime suspect any information. And if he was innocent, the less he knew about how things looked back there, the better off he would be, especially given the interrogation he was soon to go through. But he was the boy's father and Mason knew that the boy must have seen his mother, naked and beaten to a bloody pulp, laying on the floor of the family room just off the kitchen of the small one story house, right down the hall from his own room. There was no way he could not have seen her.

Mason looked at him and said, "He must have seen her Jim. There is no way he would have gone to the Bacons with out at least having looked in the family room. And if he did, he saw her. He must have."

"How about Mike and the baby. How did they get to the Bacons'?"

"Ken Bacon went and got them after Billy came to his house. He woke Mike up. I don't think Mike saw her."

Williams just processed it all. Then he looked at Mason and said, "Are we done? Can I see my children?"

"Yeah, we're done for now Jim. Let's go in."

As the two stepped from the car, from their respective sides they turned and looked back down the street towards the mouth of Williams' driveway. The crowd was still there, watching them.

Chapter 12

They walked up to the Bacons' front porch, but as they got closer Mason took Williams by the arm.

"Wait, you've got blood on your face. The last thing the boys need to see is more blood."

The chief signaled to one of his officers and told him to go inside and ask Mrs. Bacon for a wet washcloth and a towel. While they waited, the Chief, still torn between his duties as a police officer and a human, debated what to do next.

"Look, Jim, I don't want you talking to Billy or Mike about what they did or didn't see."

As Williams started to respond, the chief cut him off. "Listen, like it or not, there is a police investigation going on here. And maybe more importantly, you've got two boys in there who may have seen their mother dead, may have seen her murdered. At this point they don't seem to want to talk about it. Maybe that's good. Maybe it's not. I just don't know. There are people better qualified than me, and maybe you, to figure out how to question them without hurting them more than they've already been hurt. But I do know I can't have you talking about any of this with them, not without at least me or a DA in the room. So you go in there and you comfort them, you do what you can to make them feel better and to try to reassure them that somehow things will get better, but Jim, I've got to stay with you. And you cannot ask them about what happened over at your house."

The officer returned with the washcloth and towel and Williams cleaned himself up. He didn't say anything. He just methodically scrubbed his face and then his hands.

As he finished, he looked at Mason. Mason pointed to his own left nostril and Williams scrubbed there again. Mason nodded and they went up the front step and inside.

Charlie

Ken Bacon met them at the door. He too didn't know how to greet Williams. He didn't know whether he was meeting a victim or a murderer.

Williams extended his hand and, looking the older man straight in the eye, said, "Thank you, Ken. Thank you for looking out for my children.'

Bacon looked him square back and seemed to make up his mind. He took his hand and shook it, placing his other on Williams' shoulder. "I'm sorry, Jim. I'm so, so sorry."

There was an awkward silence and the men released their grips. With his other hand still on Williams' shoulder, Bacon gently guided him towards the back of the house. "Billy and Mike are in back with Helen and a few of the neighbor ladies. The baby's asleep in our room."

Williams nodded and led them down the hall, through the kitchen and down the steps into the already-crowded family room.

Mike was the first to see his father and when he did, he ran to him. Williams squatted to meet the boy and easily scooped him up. Holding him in one arm, the father squeezed him tight and kissed the top of his head as he walked back towards his oldest son.

When their eyes met, Williams' heart sank. Billy looked at him with fear and hatred. He cowered back into the couch, trying to get as far away from his father as he possibly could.

The boy's reaction startled everyone in the room. Anyone there who had previously given him the benefit of the doubt now had to believe that Jim Williams had murdered his wife and that his eleven year-old son had witnessed it.

For a few seconds that seemed like minutes, everyone was perfectly still. Then Williams moved forward, trying to reconnect with his son. At first the boy continued to cower, then with a sense of resolve that seemed as serious as his father's, he stood and let himself be hugged.

Chapter 13

Chief Mason politely cleared everyone except the Bacons and the Williams from the room. But even as the neighbor ladies left, he knew that the story of Billy's reaction to his father would spread through the town and that any public presumption of innocence would soon be gone.

He let Williams sit with his sons but remained within earshot. Williams was comforting but serious with the boys. Billy remained attentive and polite, but he clearly was being extremely cautious. After a while, Mike asked where his mother was. Jim looked up at the chief who barely nodded in response.

Williams pulled the boy closer to him on the couch and with an arm around his shoulder quietly said, "Mike, Mommy, well, she died. She is in heaven,"

As the younger boy burst into tears and asked a spate of questions, Chief Mason watched Billy. He looked and carried himself like his father. He listened to his father try to explain to his brother that his mother was gone. The boy watched with a cold detachment that a grown man five times his age couldn't muster.

Jim held his weeping son tight and reached out to Billy, pulling him to his side. The boy moved to him, and let him hold him, but he gave nothing back.

Ken Bacon coughed a manufactured cough and walked into the family room. "Matt, Susan's parents are walking up to the house."

When Billy heard that he broke from his father's arm and ran to the side door and out into the driveway. The rest of the group followed him out and saw him run up to his grandmother and into her arms. They both burst into tears.

Williams put Mike down and he too ran to his grandparents, jumping into his crouching grandfather's embrace. The four of them stayed like that for a moment and then Jim approached.

Emily and Frank Anderson were both in their mid sixties. They lived thirty minutes outside of Philadelphia and had just spent about three or four hours driving across the state, helplessly knowing only that their daughter had been murdered. The boys presence left them still helpless to ask the questions they must have been discussing or at least thinking, but it also gave them an outlet for their feelings, a positive one. They hugged the boys tightly, switching from child to child. Williams stood nearby but alone, watching, grateful for what they could give to his boys.

After a bit, Frank stood and walked up to his son-in-law. He put his hand on the back of Jim's shoulder and led him to the back of the driveway. He looked over his own shoulder, surprised to see the police officer following them,

"Frank, this is Matt Mason, the local police chief."

As the two men shook hands, Anderson pulled the officer further down the driveway as far away from his grandchildren as he could. Addressing both men, he said, "What happened?" And to his son-in-law, "Where were you? Why didn't you protect her?"

Mason realized that it hadn't occurred to him that his son-in-law might be the murderer.

The Chief was still in the same dilemma. He wanted to explain to the father exactly what had happened, but he did not want to discuss the case in front of Williams. He looked at Williams and saw a sense of shame on his normally emotionless face. Whether it was shame for not being there to protect her or for having killed her, the chief didn't know.

"I'm sorry, Frank. I don't know what happened."

"Jim, why don't you give me a minute with your father-in-law? Let me explain what we know."

Anderson's confusion increased as he watched his son-in-law step away.

"Mr. Anderson, this morning at about 6 AM your grandson Billy knocked on the Bacons' front door. He said he couldn't find his mother. While Helen Bacon watched Billy and Ken, Mr. Bacon went over to your daughter's house. He knocked on the front door and got no answer, so he went around to the side door. He knocked on that door, too, and again got no answer. He then looked in through the window and saw your daughter on the floor. She was dead, sir, bludgeoned to death."

From experience Mason knew it was best to just deliver the facts. He let this sink in for a moment and then continued.

"After he saw the body, Mr. Bacon wanted to call the police right away, but he didn't want to go into the house. So he ran back to his house. He told Mrs. Bacon to call us, the police. Then he ran back to your daughter's house to get the other two boys. He ran back over there and went in the front door. It was locked so he broke a windowpane and unlocked it and grabbed the boys."

The father looked up at him. "Did the boys see her?"

"We have to assume that Billy did. We don't think Mike did, but at this point we can't be sure."

The man's shoulders slumped.

"Mr. Bacon took Mike and the baby back to his house. We got here about ten or fifteen minutes later at about 6:45. We found your daughter."

He gave Anderson a moment to gather his thoughts.

"Where was Jim?"

"He was hunting, in the woods near Concord."

"Who did this?"

"We don't know, sir."

Anderson looked over to his daughter's house, which he could see through the woods. Then he looked up the driveway to his wife and grandchildren and then to his son-in-law. Then he looked back at the officer.

"You don't think . . ." The man's voice trailed off, he couldn't bring himself to say it, to think it.

"We don't know who did it, sir."

After another minute or two of questioning, Anderson and Mason made their way back up the driveway, joining Williams and walking towards the boys.

Anderson looked at his son-in-law. He refused to believe he could have done this. While he was not close to his son-in-law, he had to admit he respected him. He was an intense man. When his daughter had first started seeing him, like any father, he had viewed the young man with a critical eye. At that point, Williams had recently returned from two tours in Viet Nam, in the infantry. His daughter met him at a hospital in Philadelphia where she worked as a technician.

From what Anderson knew, Jim had been shot in the shoulder. He had been awarded both the Purple Heart and the Distinguished Service Cross. There were rumors that he had been considered for the Congressional Medal of Honor. As a World War II combat veteran himself, Anderson knew that the Distinguished Service Cross didn't come cheap and he respected the boy's record, what he knew of it, and also his reluctance to discuss it.

After he got out of the hospital, Williams had stayed in Philadelphia and found a job in construction. He and Susan dated and eventually she brought him out to their suburban home to meet them. From the outset, he had been quiet and reserved. The Andersons were concerned by his lack of a college education, but they had to admit that he was a hard-working, serious young man, and it was always clear that in his own quiet way, he loved their daughter dearly. They had always thought that while he might not be the most fun person she could marry, he would always work hard and look after her. They thought she would always be safe with him.

The irony of that struck Anderson hard and he viewed his son-in-law warily.

Quietly, he asked, "What in the world happened? Who could have done this, Jim?"

Chief Mason was standing nearby and Anderson turned to him and said, "Excuse me, Chief, um."

"Mason, Matt Mason, sir,"

"Yes, sorry, well, Chief Mason, could you give me and Jim a minute?"

Mason shifted on his feet. "Actually, sir, I can't."

Mason didn't want to specifically say that their son-in-law was the prime suspect, but neither could he allow Williams the opportunity to talk before he was properly questioned.

"I'm afraid Jim and I have to go down to the station. We need to ask him a lot of questions so that we can figure out who did this. He might not know it, but Jim here can probably help us a lot, sir."

"I wanted to get him together with his children, but now that you and Mrs. Anderson are here, I really have to question him in more detail so that we can start trying to get to the bottom of this."

Williams looked at the chief. He knew the fine line Mason was walking and knew that he was probably the primary suspect. He was grateful for the deft manner in which the chief was handling things.

Williams hugged his mother-in-law and his sons, explaining that he was going to go with the chief for a while. The Andersons saw how Billy reacted when his father hugged him. The boy had always worshipped his father. Frank looked at his wife as the boy winced. He wondered if she, too, already suspected him. He hoped not. The thought was more than she would be able to bear.

Chapter 14

Mason had a young officer drive Williams down to the station while he returned to the crime scene.

The coroner was doing forensic work, checking for prints and boot marks. Susan Williams was not the best of housekeepers and clearly there would be many, many prints to sort through.

He made sure the crime scene was stable and headed back to the station. It was now 3:20 PM. If Williams wasn't the killer, whoever was had had three to six hours to cover his tracks and about eight more to get away.

Chapter 15

Over the next several hours both Mason and the county District Attorney Jerry Miller had questioned Williams again and again. They got very little in the way of new information.

What they did know was on the evening of Susan's death both the Bacons and the neighbors on the other side, the Landers, had heard the Williams arguing. From what they had heard, the argument or at least the yelling, had been pretty one sided, with Susan as the more vocal participant.

The argument was at about 7PM. After that every thing they had came from Williams and from the testimony of Billy and Mike. With their grandfather present and notably, with their father's permission, Miller and the chief had questioned the boys one at a time in the Bacons' family room.

The boys' stories were similar. Their dad had gotten home at about 5:30. They had dinner at about 6, all five of them and then at about 8:30 they went to bed. As the boys said he did most nights, Jim read them a chapter of *The Yearling* and then tucked them in.

The boys did remember hearing their parents quarreling, which they said happened a lot. They said no one else had been around.

When asked about why he had woken up so early and why he went over to the Bacons' house, Billy simply said he couldn't find his mom. While Miller and the Chief had wanted to press him on the matter, they thought better of it, partly out of respect for the boy and partly because of the look that they were getting from his grandfather.

After the interviews, the men really only had one suspect and it was Williams. From the look on the victim's father's face, it was clear he had reached the same conclusion.

Walking from the Bacons' house out to their cars at the foot of the driveway, the chief and the DA discussed what to do.

"What do you think, Matt?"

"Well, the evidence all points to Williams, but in my gut, I don't know, Jerry. What do you think?"

"You're right, the evidence says Williams. He was the only one home. The dogs didn't bark. If there had been a stranger there, they would have been barking. Listen to them now."

Miller paused and the men listened to the dogs' constant barking at the officers in the driveway. They hadn't stopped for hours.

Miller continued. "The neighbors heard them arguing and the Landers were sitting on their screened-in porch until about 10. If the dogs had barked at a stranger, they would have heard it."

"I agree."

"Then we have the gap. From 9:00 when Williams read to the boys and their mom came in and kissed them goodnight until about 6:30 when Ken Bacon found the body. There was plenty of time for Williams to kill his wife and drive to Concord. The officer up there didn't find him until what, 11:30 this morning?"

Mason nodded.

"Williams says he left at about 10 last night. The Landers don't remember hearing him go, but that is about the time they went inside. So he may or may not have left about then. The coroner's initial estimate of the time of death is between 10PM and 1 AM. No one on the street saw him leave and no one noticed any other cars coming or going. That's not conclusive either way, but it all points to Williams, Matt."

"I agree, Jerry. The evidence all points to him, but I'm just not sure."

Miller and Mason had worked together for years and the DA had a healthy respect for the chief's gut. "Outline why for me Matt."

"Okay, I'll do this chronologically. First, I talked with the officer who found him in the woods, an experienced cop from the Concord PD named Kipp. Like every police officer in the region, Kipp had been told that Mason's wife had been murdered and that he might be hunting in his area. He was also told that if he found Williams, he should approach with caution.

"Kipp said that while he found William's truck, it was Williams who found him out in the woods. He said Williams had appeared to have been surprised and shocked when he heard that there was a problem at his house. It was Williams who led Kipp back to his car.

"Kipp said that when they were walking out of the woods he was a little lost and nervous about walking in front of Williams with Williams carrying a hunting rifle. Williams apparently sensed his nervousness and voluntarily handed his rifle, actually, I think it was a shotgun, to Kipp and then led him back to his truck. The whole way Williams pressed him for more information, but as I said Kipp told him only what he knew, except for the approach-with-caution part. Then when they got to his truck Williams apparently just tossed his keys to one of the state troopers there. Whoever did this had to have been covered in blood, Jerry. Even if he cleaned himself up at the house, when he got in his car or truck there must have been at least the possibility of some blood on him and some of that blood would surely have been left in the car. Even if he had cleaned his vehicle, the murderer would have known that there might still be some trace of evidence left behind. But as I said, when he was asked, Williams just tossed the state trooper up in Concord his van keys. Kipp said it looked like the act of an innocent man. That it looked as though it never even occurred to Williams that his van might somehow be incriminating.

"Between hiking out and driving down here, Kipp accompanied Williams and the troopers on their trip back, they spent about four hours together. By the time we talked Kipp had spoken with some of my guys and the state troopers here. They told him that Mrs. Williams had been brutally murdered. Kipp told me that if Jim Williams was the murderer, then he was the coolest character he had ever come across.

"Next. I am the one who told Jim how Susan had been murdered. Jerry, I can tell you right now, he was shocked. I watched him closely and saw two distinct reactions, first shock and then rage. I don't know if you know, Jerry, but this guy is a bona fide war hero. He has done some serious stuff, and I know that works both ways here, but when he heard his wife had been murdered, he looked like he wanted to kill some one.

"Next, and this part is just between you and me, Jerry, for now at least." Mason paused, gathering his thoughts. "Over the past few years, there have been a few times when Susan has gotten into trouble."

The DA gave him a surprised, questioning look.

"She is a party girl, Jerry, drinking and fooling around. About two years ago, the chief over in Lewisburg called me at about two in the morning, called me at home. He told me he had a lady from my town in his station, Susan Williams. She had wrecked her car and was drunk. The chief asked me about her and I said she had kids, no record. We decided to give her the benefit of the doubt. I went and got her. Jerry, she was dressed for fun and she was one good-looking woman. Anyway, I drove her home that night. By then she was sober. When we got to her house her husband met us in the driveway.

Charlie

He didn't seem all that surprised to see her like that. He didn't get mad, just thanked me, asked about her car and helped her back into the house. I had a sense that he had been through this before."

"Is there any record of this?"

"No, I didn't see any point. I made Jim promise not to make an insurance claim on the car and told him that so long as he did not make a claim, I'd keep it between us. And until now that's just what I have done."

"So you're saying there might be someone else out there? A lover or something?"

"I'm saying that it is possible."

"But, that could be a motive for Williams."

"Yeah, you're right, it could. Or it could mean that there is someone else out there."

"I agree."

"And then finally, Jerry, I don't know Williams well, but everything I do know, I like. This guy is simply a quiet family man. He works his tail off and he carries himself in a way I have always admired."

"So what do you want to do?"

"Well, that is the problem I have. I don't see how we can let him go right now."

The DA looked at the chief with surprise. "After everything you just said you want to arrest him now? Why not wait, try to get more information?"

Mason nodded towards the Bacons' house. "Because of those kids. Look, in spite of my gut, the evidence points to him. If he is the murderer, there is no way that we can let him be alone with the only potential witnesses to his crime. The oldest boy saw his mother this morning. There is no doubt in my mind. She was naked and beaten to a pulp, Jerry. You saw her. No kid should have to see that. At the very least he saw that. There is no chance he would have gone to the Bacons' house without having looked for her. And maybe Mike saw her, too. I don't think he did, but I can't be sure. So if they are lying or blocking out having seen her body, they may also be lying or blocking out having seen or heard their father murder her."

"Jeez, the poor kids. It will take years to undo what they have seen, if it ever can be undone."

"You should have seen the look Billy gave his father when he first saw him this afternoon. If he doesn't know his father killed her, he at least thinks it."

"So there is no way we can allow him to be alone with those kids. And the only way we can do that with certainty is to arrest him."

"What if we have the grandparents stay with them?"

"You're the lawyer, you tell me. Even if they watch the boys, unless we arrest him it's his right to watch over them. We can't risk that, Jerry. Do you think we have enough to arrest him?"

The DA thought it over. "Yeah, I think so. It's Saturday so we can hold him over the weekend. It will give us some time to put together our case for the grand jury."

"Now we have to figure out what to do with the kids. They should be with their grandparents. They're obviously close and those kids need some one who really cares about them."

"Where are they from?"

"Just outside Philly. We need to find a local place for them to stay. They can't stay in the Williams place."

"Okay, let's hold him on suspicion of murder. Why don't you radio the station and have someone read him his rights and then lock him up?"

"No, I think I'll go back and do it myself. Then I'll come back here and try to figure out about the kids."

Chapter 16

When Mason got back to station he had Williams, who had been waiting in a conference room, brought into his office.

The chief stood when the officer brought Williams in. The men shook hands and Mason pointed to one of the two seats in front of his desk.

"Have a seat please, Mr. Williams."

As Williams sat down, the chief sat behind his desk.

Williams spoke first.

"Do you have any idea who did this, Chief Mason?"

"Frankly, I was hoping you could help me with that."

Williams looked up at him, his expression giving away nothing. "I have no idea."

Mason and Williams were both quiet men and both better at listening than talking. Finally the chief spoke.

"Look, Mr. Williams, Jim, this is a murder case. The last time you and I met officially, we were sort of working around the law. But this is different. Your wife was brutally murdered. And to be honest, the only person we can even consider at this point is you."

There was no look of surprise or shock on Williams' face, nor any of indignation. The chief did not take this as a sign of anything other than Williams' intelligence. He had weighed the facts and reached the same conclusion the chief had, that he was their best suspect.

After another pause, this time it was Williams who spoke first.

"I did not kill my wife."

"Then who did?"

"I don't know."

Again, the two paused.

"Look, Mr. Williams, the last time we met, well, it was clear that your wife was, well, stepping out. And to be honest, from your reaction that night, I had the sense that it wasn't her first time."

Williams just looked at him, his face stone.

"Was your wife seeing someone else?"

He didn't respond.

"Look, Mr. Williams, unless you can give me a reason not to, in about thirty seconds I am going to arrest you for suspicion of murder."

He paused and let that sink in. Still there was no reaction.

"What did you two argue about last night?"

"I told you, Chief Mason. It was about money."

"Is that all?"

He nodded.

"Was she seeing someone else?"

He held the chief's gaze for a moment and then looked down to the floor.

"I did not kill my wife. But I don't know what I can say that will convince you that I didn't. So if you are going to arrest me, go ahead."

Mason looked at him for a moment and then said, "James Williams, I am arresting you for suspicion of murder." The chief then read him his rights. Williams acknowledged that he understood those rights.

The chief rose to lead him out, but as he started to rise Williams stopped him.

"Chief, what about my kids?"

The chief's tone softened. "What do you want us to do with them?"

"They should be with Susan's parents."

"That's what I thought, too. But the question is where."

"Not at our house?"

"No, not for a while at least. It is a crime scene."

Williams thought for a while and said. "Someone should talk with Billy. Someone qualified. There is no way he would have gone over to the Bacon's unless he saw something. He sometimes sits for his brothers for short periods. He wouldn't have gone to the Bacons' unless something was wrong. He should stay with his grandparents. They all should. If I can't be with them, someone who loves them should."

Mason's instincts again told him that he was not sitting across from a murderer.

"I'll go see your in-laws as soon as we finish. We will find a place for the five of them to stay together. Are they still young enough to handle this? I mean, with the baby and everything?"

"Yeah, I think so. Helen Bacon watches the kids a lot. Maybe she could help too, especially with the baby."

"Okay, I'll see what I can do and I'll let you know. Is there anything else?"

"Yeah, my dogs. The two at the house and the third is with my van up in Concord. Officer Kipp said someone from his department would drive it and my dog down here."

Mason had been on the phone with the Concord PD earlier in the afternoon. They had the truck and the dog at the station. The county forensic team was going over the truck, looking for traces of blood and once Officer Kipp got back up there, he and some of the other officers were going to try to retrace his and Williams steps to see if they could find any evidence he may have tried to hide there.

"That reminds me, the Concord PD says your dog won't stop barking. And the two at your house are driving everyone nuts."

Williams nodded and thought for a minute. "Just tell the guys up in Concord and at my house to calmly say 'Charlie.' They'll be quiet after that."

"Really? Why?"

"In addition to hunting dogs, they're watch dogs. I take work wherever I can get it, Chief. Sometimes I'm away for a night or two. I've trained them to bark when strangers are around, to protect Susan and the boys."

He looked suddenly crushed, realizing that his training hadn't worked.

And then his thoughts met the Chief's.

"Did anyone else know about saying 'Charlie?'"

"Only Susan."

"The dogs weren't barking last night. Either there wasn't a stranger there or Susan or someone else said 'Charlie.'"

Mason rose again and led Williams to the basement, where the cells were. Everyone in the station watched them. The chief pointed to the first cell and the officer at the desk outside the cells opened it. Williams walked in and the officer closed it behind him.

"I'll take care of your dogs. Should I leave them with your family or take them to my place?"

Williams smiled a small smile and said, "Thank you. My mother-in-law doesn't really like the dogs. It might be easier if you took them, if you don't mind."

"I will. And I'll let you know where your family is staying."

Again the two men shook hands, this time through the bars. The officer behind the chief watched, seeing something he had never seen before.

Chapter 17

As he drove back to the Bacons' house, the chief tried to figure out how he would explain to the Andersons that he had arrested their son-in-law for the murder of their daughter. He knew that word of the arrest would be spreading through town rapidly and he hoped he could beat the news to the Bacons'.

While he wanted to go through the crime scene and the surrounding area one last time before it got dark, he knew he had to see the Andersons first.

He pulled onto the Williams' normally quiet dead end street, Milmar Court, and was surprised to see a circus there. There were cars lining the entire street and as he turned the bend near the Williams' driveway, he saw about fifty people gathered on Milmar, across from the Williams' driveway. He turned on his lights and nudged through the crowd.

As Chief Mason passed, several of the people yelled out questions. He just nodded and ignored them and drove slowly to the Bacon's driveway. He parked at the foot and told one of the two officers there to go over to the Williams' driveway and to move the crowd back off of Milmar. He knew if he got them that far back, most would go home.

Then he reluctantly made his way down the driveway to the Bacons' house. When he was halfway down, Ken Bacon walked out to meet him. Bacon stopped him and pulled him away from the house.

"Is it true? Did you arrest Jim?"

"Yes."

"Did he kill her?"

"Ken, we are holding him on suspicion of murder. That's really all I can say. How did you find out?"

"It's all over town. One of my wife's friends called her."

"Do the Andersons know?"

"No, we didn't want to tell them until we were sure. Is that why you're here?"

The chief nodded. "Yeah, I guess I better tell them. How are the boys doing?"

"Not too well and neither is Mrs. Anderson, though she's doing a good job of hiding it from the kids."

"Well, we, Mr. Williams and I, we discussed it and we were hoping that they would stay with the kids until we can sort this all out. We just have to find a place for them to stay."

Mason looked at Bacon, realizing that he too had seen the inside of the Williams' house and knew there was a lot to be done before the kids or the Andersons could go near the place.

"My wife and I were also discussing it and we thought that they could stay here for a while. We were thinking Jim and the kids, but it doesn't matter, Mr. and Mrs. Anderson and the kids can stay here. Helen and I can get a room at the Holiday Inn for a week or so. We figured we could come and go during the day and maybe, if Mrs. Anderson wants, Helen can help her with the kids. She has spent a lot of time with them and really loves them."

"That is awfully kind of you, Ken. Are you sure?"

Bacon waved him off. "Let's see how the Andersons feel about it, but you go ahead and offer it on our behalf, Matt."

The chief smiled and shook the man's hand. Together they made their way up the driveway and in the side door.

When they walked into the family room, everyone looked up at them. Mr. and Mrs. Anderson and Mrs. Bacon were sitting at the kitchen table with the boys. Mrs. Anderson was holding the five-month old baby, feeding him from a bottle. The rest were involved in some sort of a card game.

Seeing the chief, Mr. Anderson immediately put down his cards and stood up. He walked over to the officer, effectively cutting him off from the room. The chief followed his lead and together they walked through the kitchen to the front of the house.

"Where's Jim? What is going on over there?" He pointed towards his daughter's house.

"Mr. Anderson, we're holding your son-in-law."

Anderson literally staggered. He made his way to the couch in the living room and sat, slumping over with his elbows on his knees, his forehead resting in his palms. Without looking up, he asked, "Did he do it?"

From behind him, Chief Mason heard a gasp.

"Did who do it?"

The chief turned and saw Mrs. Anderson standing behind him. Before he could answer Mr. Anderson stood and cut him off, walking towards his wife. "Honey, they have arrested Jim."

Mrs. Anderson looked at him and burst into tears. He took her into his arms and simply held her, almost supporting her. The chief wanted to give them a minute, but was sure they would have questions and didn't feel he should leave.

Seemingly reading his thoughts, the Andersons made their way back to the couch and sat facing him. He sat in the chair opposite from them, barely on the seat, leaning in to them.

"Did he do it?"

The chief paused for a moment and then responded. "I don't know, sir. I honestly don't know. But the evidence points to him. I had to arrest him, Mr. Anderson."

"If you're not sure, why did you arrest him?"

Mason couldn't believe the mess he had gotten himself into. He wanted to comfort them, not to completely crucify their son-in-law in their eyes, and instead he was now going to have to make him look worse.

Trying still to obfuscate, he responded, "We had to, sir."

"Why, if you're not sure?"

The chief didn't know what to do. He didn't want to describe the brutality of the crime any more than he wanted to talk about the possibility of him harming the boys.

"Sir, with a murder, we just can't take chances. Your son-in-law has no record, no history of violence. He is, as you know, a war hero and a model citizen. I don't want you two to think he is guilty. Until we know otherwise you have to believe he is innocent. But with a crime of this nature I have to follow the evidence. And at this point, the evidence leads us to him."

Mrs. Anderson spoke. "But what about the boys? They worship him. What are we going to tell them? Poor Billy and Mike have been through so much. Frank told me about your conversation, what Billy must have seen. They need their father."

"Mr. Williams and I spoke about this. It is his wish, if you are willing, that until we straighten this out, that you take care of the boys. Can you do that? Will you?"

They both started to respond, but Mr. Anderson let her finish. "Yes, of course. But where will we stay? Should we take them back to our house? No, the boys will have to eventually go back to school."

Thinking out loud, she went on, "We should try, somehow, to make their lives get back to normal as soon as we can." With that it seemed to again hit her that her daughter had been murdered, that she was gone.

Holding his wife to him, Mr. Anderson asked, "Can we move back into Susan's house?"

"No, not for a while. For now, it's a crime scene, and after that, if only for the boys' sake, we should probably go slowly. For the immediate future the Bacons want the five of you to stay here. They are going to get a room at the hotel in town. During the day Mrs. Bacon has offered to help you, only if you want her help. I think she sits for the boys a lot. She clearly is very fond of them."

"That is extremely thoughtful of them."

"They just want to help. We all do. I will have an officer bring over some of the baby's things and some of the boys' things, too. For the time being, if you need anything from the house, just let me know."

"What about those dogs?" Even as she asked Chief Mason could hear them barking in the background.

The chief allowed himself a tiny smile. "They're coming home with me." Then he thought to himself, *though I haven't told my wife yet.*

Mr. Anderson stood, then helped his wife up. Mason stood, too.

"Listen, Chief Mason, my wife and I appreciate what you are doing, everything. But there is something you need to know. Jim Williams did not kill my daughter. He is quiet and hard to get to know, but he is a good man, a really good man. And he loves . . . loved my Susan with all his heart. So I don't want you to get into the mindset of proving that he killed her. Do you understand? You have to figure out who did do this. Because right now you have the wrong guy."

"I understand, sir, I really do. And I hope you are right."

Mason talked with Mrs. Anderson and Mrs. Bacon and together they compiled a list of things the chief should have sent over from the house. With that he left, deciding to go through the backyard to the Williams', to both avoid the crowd out on the street and to get a sense of things from back there.

Charlie

The dogs were still barking. But he could also hear his men and the troopers yelling at them. There was no doubt that if a stranger had approached last night, the neighbors would have heard it.

He made his way through the woods into the Williams' backyard. Aside from the dirt circles around where the dogs' chains were anchored, everything was in perfect order. The yard was meticulous.

One of his men and a trooper were standing near the dogs, trying uselessly to quiet them. The chief smiled and decided to try a little test.

"What's wrong, men?"

"Chief, I'm about ready to shoot these two mutts. They have been barking all day. Honestly all day."

The state trooper nodded his agreement. The chief looked at them and said, "Let me see what I can do."

The younger men sort of laughed and watched as the thirty-seven year old chief made his way to the dogs. The dogs barked at him more and more aggressively as he approached. When he was just beyond their reach, he squatted and extended his hands. Still barking the dog's lunged trying to get to him. In a very low voice, he whispered, "Easy boys, easy."

The dogs kept barking and became more and more agitated. Mason looked over his shoulder and saw the two officers smiling, having tried to calm the dogs many times themselves.

He turned back facing them again and whispered, "Easy boys" and then more quietly, so that the officers could not hear him, he whispered, "Charlie."

Instantly the dogs sat and stopped barking. Mason rose and walked up between them, offering each the back of a downturned hand. The dogs licked his hands and wagged their tails, panting happily. He petted them both and turned to see the two dumbfounded officers behind him. He smiled and said, "What's the problem guys? They seem awfully nice to me."

The officers just shook their heads. The chief told his own officer to come forward and he got the dogs comfortable with him. He decided not to tell him about "Charlie" both because he liked the thought of his men thinking he could handle any situation and more importantly, because it might become a significant part of the case against the killer, if it wasn't Williams.

With the dogs now calmed, he made his way back to the house. He was surprised to see that Mrs. Williams' body was still in place, covered with a sheet, but still in the same place where it had been when he got there about eleven hours earlier. The county coroner, Paul Milton, seemed to read his thoughts. He said, "There are so many foot prints in the area, I'm just trying to catalogue everything before I have the body removed. But the stretcher is coming now."

"Before you do, let's clear the area and try to walk through what you think may have happened."

He turned to the officers just outside the door and told them to get everyone up to the front of the house, no closer than the front yard.

Then he walked over to the body and, trying to remain dispassionate, pulled off the sheet that was covering it. He folded the sheet and placed it by the door, then said to the coroner, "Okay, walk me through what you think happened."

Standing by the door with the chief, Milton began, "There is no sign of forced entry so either this door was unlocked, which it may well have been, or she let the killer in."

The chief thought about Ken Bacon having found the door locked and then he himself finding it unlocked shortly afterward. He made a mental note to talk to Bacon about that, but didn't say anything to Milton.

The coroner walked carefully around the body over to the three wide steps that led down from the kitchen. "I think this is where the first blow was struck." From the base of the steps he pointed to a splattering of blood and other, thicker goo against the half-wall on the left side of the steps. "I think the murderer was behind her on the top step and swung at her, striking the back of her head."

Milton walked to the body and pointed to the back, top of her skull. "I think this is that first blow. Then as she was going down, I guess he hit her a couple more times on her head and back."

Trailing his pointed finger from the spot by the foot of the steps over the three feet to the body, he went on, "Those blows must have knocked her over and she fell to where she is now. I think he hit her five or six more times as she was lying there." He pointed to the corpse. There was a lot of blood splattered around the outline of her body.

"Now this is the weird part . . ."

He squatted beside the corpse and pointed to the remains of her nightgown, which were on the floor a few feet further into the family room. He pointed at the back of the nightgown.

"Do you see these blood stains? It looks to me as though she had this on during the initial stage of the beating. You can tell from the stains that when he was hitting her it splattered here."

Again he pointed to stains along the upper back of the gown.

"So she was wearing it when he first hit her. And then, and this is the weird part, the killer apparently tore off her gown."

He looked up at Mason.

"There is no evidence of rape or recent intercourse, though I will know more when I get her to the morgue."

The chief nodded.

He pointed to the spot where her body still was. "The fatal blows occurred here. I counted five blows to her back and the back of her skull. I can't tell the order, but I'm guessing she was dead long before he finished."

Mason just listened, wanting to hear only the coroner's thoughts.

"There are, in my mind, two contradicting bits of evidence here, Matt. On the one hand it doesn't seem to me that a man who had been married to a woman for over twelve years would rip her nightgown off after he had already almost killed her. You see what I mean? To want to see a woman's naked body after all of this violence, well, why would someone who must have seen that body so many times bother? From the amount of blood on the back of her gown, it stands to reason she must have been almost dead when he ripped it from her. It just doesn't seem like something a husband of many years would do. On the other hand, whoever did this was obviously in fit of rage. That could be a husband. I'm not saying it has to be, but it certainly could be. Anyway, after he killed her here, the killer smeared the prints on the hammer and simply dropped it. There are several sets of footprints between the body and the door. I'm guessing this set belonged to the killer." He pointed to some nondescript footprints, the most prevalent ones, around the body and the steps. There was a smeared spot near the foot of the steps. "It looks as though he wiped his feet here."

"I think the other sets belong to you and your men and or the neighbor who found the body this morning. Those sets were fainter and were dirt, not blood. It is going to be difficult to sort this all out, but I've taken a ton of pictures. That's what's taking me so long."

Mason knew that Bacon hadn't been in this room, but for now he didn't want to interrupt the coroner's thoughts.

"Is there anything else?"

"Yeah, dinner dishes are by the sink. Looks like there were four people who ate, probably just the family."

They looked at the dishes. There was dried food on them.

"As you can see the plates were scraped and placed by the sink. They haven't been rinsed. There is no evidence that the killer cleaned himself up here in this sink or in either of the other two sinks. It seems as though whoever did this left with what must have been a lot of blood still on him."

The chief agreed. Looking back into the family room, he added, "He must have had blood all over him."

"Other than that there is the broken front windowpane, which I gather the neighbor broke when he came back to get the other boys. And there is one other thing."

He motioned for Mason to follow him up the steps, along the right side. Past the steps on the kitchen floor there was another set of footprints, small barefoot footprints. They led to the center of the kitchen, turned back to face the family room and then led up the hallway to the front door. The broken glass from the pane lay on top of some of the prints.

"Those must be the oldest son Billy's prints. If there was any question as to whether he had seen his mother, it is gone, Matt. The poor kid."

The chief just shook his head. At least there was only one set of smaller footprints. There was still hope that the second son, Mike, hadn't seen the body.

"Do you have any other thoughts?"

Milton hesitated then said, "Yeah, I don't know what to make of this, and it may be nothing, but look at this."

He led Mason back into the family room, over to Susan's body. He lifted the sheet he had replaced from her side and exposed her buttocks. He took a wooden depressor from his coat and pointed to a small mark on the left cheek. The chief bent down and looked closely. There was dried blood over a lot of her back and backside, but when he looked closely he saw she had a tattoo, a small flower on her cheek, very close to the cleft.

"That is a pretty personal spot for a tattoo, Matt. I didn't expect to see that."

The chief didn't comment. He just nodded and pulled the sheet back over her.

Chapter 18

After he and the coroner left the family room, Mason had his officers take the dogs and put them in his truck. Milton and his staff were removing Susan's body, but other than that, the chief had decided to leave the scene exactly intact for another day or two.

On his way back to the office, he radioed in and told the desk officer to find him two leashes or if they couldn't find those, two four or five-foot lengths of rope.

The officer met him in the parking lot and the chief leashed the dogs and walked them over to the grass at the side of the lot before heading inside. The dogs were happily sniffing around, but never once pulled on their leads.

He took the dogs through the station into his office and closed the door behind him. Then he simply dropped the leashes and let them wander about. He sat at his desk and watched as they sniffed around. He quietly said sit and both immediately sat and then lay down, resting quietly.

He took the list that Mrs. Anderson and Mrs. Bacon had put together from his pocket and dialed his wife.

"Hi, honey, it's me."

His wife Maryanne had heard about the murder and the subsequent arrest, but she hadn't wanted to bother him on what she was sure was the busiest day of his career.

"How is it going?"

"I don't know. I'll tell you what I'm thinking when I get home. It's a mess."

Maryanne knew that while he often kept things to himself, with tough issues he sometimes laid out his thoughts for her and used her as a respected sounding board. Generally, though, he shielded her from the more grizzly cases.

"I do need you to do something for me, though."

"Sure, what do you need, Matt?"

He explained that he had promised to deliver some things to the Bacon's house from the Williams' house, but that he had subsequently decided not to touch anything in the house for another day or two. She happily agreed to go to the Kmart and get everything on the list and also two extra toothbrushes in case the Andersons forgot theirs in haste that morning.

Mason knew she would be good with the Andersons and the Bacons and to be honest he wanted to get her involved. The boys were going to need a lot of support and he knew that she would see that and help him to see to their needs.

While she was in a good and helpful mood, the husband of twelve years added, "Oh, and Maryanne, while you're there could you pick up three dog bowls, and some dog food?"

She laughed. For years he and their two kids had wanted a dog, but she had resisted because she knew that she would be the one who had to train and care for it.

"Three dog bowls? Matt Mason, what have you done?"

He heard the mock madness in her voice and laughed, loving her as much as ever.

"I told Jim Williams I would watch them for him. His in-laws and the Bacons have enough on their plate. It seemed like the least I could do."

Maryanne dropped her feigned anger when she heard the way he said Jim Williams' name. Like everyone else in town, she had heard he had been arrested. But she thought she sensed a tone of sympathy for him in her husband's voice. Again she resisted the urge to question him about the specifics of the case and instead asked, "Okay, and just what do three . . . three dogs eat?"

He laughed and said, "I'm guessing a lot. I'll be home in a couple of hours. Do you want me to pick up some burgers on the way home? By the time you do everything you have to, I may beat you home."

"No, I made some stew. Just heat it up if you beat me home. And Matt?"

"Yeah?"

"I don't want those dogs upstairs."

Again he laughed and said, "I'll see you at home."

Chapter 19

Mason called the chief up in Concord, a man named Ed Graber.

"Hi Chief Graber, this Matt Mason from down here in Harrison. I wanted to see if you guys found anything in William's truck."

"Yeah, hi. No, we didn't find anything. The county forensic guys went through it with a fine-toothed comb."

"Nothing, huh?"

"Yeah and the interesting thing is that they said the cab hadn't been cleaned in a while. This guy Williams keeps a pretty clean truck, but it looks like he eats lunch in his truck a lot. There were a lot of crumbs found in the driver's seat. Old crumbs."

"Hmmm."

"Yeah, and on top of that, there were lots of prints on the steering wheel. And again, while the wheel was pretty clean, there were traces of a dried substance, mostly likely mustard on the wheel. So it doesn't appear as though it was wiped clean."

"So you're saying he didn't clean the seat? That it was sort of dirty, but there was no evidence of blood or anything? And likewise the wheel was sort of dirty, but with old stuff?"

"Yeah, isn't that what I just said?"

Mason didn't really understand the guy's attitude and frankly didn't need it, but he did need his help and that of his department. So he figured he better stroke him.

"Okay, thanks, Chief. And by the way, the officer you sent down with Williams, please tell him I said thanks. He's a good cop. I appreciated his thoughts. Would you please ask him to write as thorough a report as he can on everything? I'm not trying to tell him or you how to do your job, Ed. From everything I've seen it's clear you run a first rate department. But I know he's already had a long day but even with that, the sooner he gets his thoughts on paper the better."

Again the Concord chief's attitude showed as he responded, "Yeah, he's already doing it. And by the way we tried to retrace their steps in the woods, but we didn't find anything. We went through with the hounds too and followed what we gather must have been his trail. But we didn't find anything."

"Okay, Chief, thank you. Anything else?"

"Yeah, this damn dog. We can't shut him up."

Mason looked at the two silent dogs on his floor. He considered telling the chief the "Charlie" trick, but given the attitude he'd been getting, he decided not to.

"I'm sorry. You want me to send someone up to get him?"

He paused for a minute then said, "No, that's okay. We will probably go over the van once more in the morning, so you might as well just stick with the original plan. If your guys get here anytime after around lunchtime, we should be ready release it to you. You can have the damn dog then."

Mason chuckled to himself and said, "Okay, Chief, thanks again. If there is ever anything you need, I'm your man."

"You're welcome."

They hung up and Mason sat thinking. Clearly whoever murdered Susan Williams would have been splattered with blood. There was no evidence of the murderer having cleaned himself up in the house. While it is possible he did it outside, even on the Williams' secluded driveway, it would take a pretty cool character to stand outside and clean himself with a brutally murdered corpse lying in plain view just inside. Still he made a note to check the driveway and the areas around the garden hoses for any evidence of a cleanup.

In the absence of any such evidence, whoever killed her would have been covered in blood. He could have sat on a sheet or something, but the steering wheel would have had traces of blood. And even if he had cleaned his hands, it seems likely he would have wiped down the steering wheel just to be cautious.

The more he thought about it, the more certain he was that the man he had in the cell downstairs was not the killer. And if he wasn't, then the real killer was still out there, and his trail was getting colder by the minute. Mason decided to talk to Williams one more time before he headed home.

He stood and when he did both dogs popped up, wagging their tails. He opened the door and said, "Come."

Charlie

The dogs fell in behind him and he made his way through the station, down into the basement. The guard on duty stood up when he saw the chief and was again shocked when he saw the two dogs following him. The dogs must have smelled Williams and immediately, excitedly ran to his cell.

Mason followed them and found Williams squatting and reaching through the bars, petting the happy labs.

"They're great dogs, Mr. Williams. My kids are going to love having them for a few days."

Williams stood and responded with a very guarded smile.

The chief turned to the guard, who was standing beside them. "Mike, open the cell. I'm going to go into the conference room with Mr. Williams."

"Sure, Chief."

The officer opened the cell and Mason led Williams and his dogs into the conference room opposite the cells, the one generally used for lawyer/client meetings.

The officer started to follow them in but the chief said, "We'll be fine, Mike."

Mason and Williams sat on opposite sides of a table with the dogs on Williams' side. Mason gathered his thoughts and then said, "Look, Mr. Williams, I need your help. If you didn't do this then someone else did. Do you have any idea who that might have been?"

Williams shook his head.

"Don't you want to get the guy who did this?"

"Of course I do. But I don't know who it was. I just don't know."

The chief looked at him. He realized that he was asking the question in the wrong way.

"Was your wife seeing someone else?"

Williams looked at him, but didn't respond.

"Mr. Williams, I want to find the man who killed your wife. Whether it is you or someone else, I want to get the guy. The only way that is going to happen is if I get as much information as I can. When we met a couple of years ago, I had the sense that you weren't surprised to see her dressed the way she was or having been drinking the way she was. It sure seemed as though you had seen her like that before. Was she still doing it? Was she still sometimes stepping out?"

Again, Williams remained silent.

"Look, I'm going to start checking into her habits, with or without your help. I'll check every bar and dance club within fifty miles of here. Either way I'm going to find out."

Finally Williams spoke, "Chief Mason, she's gone, she's dead. But those boys aren't. They knew her as a loving mom. Her folks knew her as a great daughter. I'm not going to do anything to change that. It's going to be hard enough for those kids, for all of them. I'm not going to do anything to hurt their memory of her."

"I understand that, but it's my job to find the killer. And to be honest, the more directed my search, the less talk that will come from it. If my officers canvas every bar within fifty miles, word of what we are doing is going to spread and so will rumors. If you can tighten the focus of the search, then chances are we can reduce the gossip. But in my experience, Mr. Williams, however we do it the truth will come out and by the time we get to court, it will all come out."

He paused to let that sink in, then continued. "So you can sit here and be quiet, trying to protect her reputation if that's what you're doing. But in doing that you are letting her killer do more and more to cover his tracks. And the public is going to want us to get someone for this. Right now, everything's pointing to you."

"I did not kill my wife."

"Then who did?"

"I don't know."

"Was she seeing someone else?"

"I don't know."

"Do you think she might have been?"

Williams was quiet for a minute. He seemed to be making a decision. The chief waited him out.

Finally Mason asked again, "Was you wife seeing someone?"

Williams paused again then looked up to the chief and shrugged his shoulders.

The chief looked at him, frustrated. He stood to leave. Williams stood too and the dogs immediately rose.

Seeing the dogs Mason stopped and asked, "Can I bring them in the house?"

"Yeah, I generally don't, but Susan does when she's home alone."

The impact of his words stuck them both.

"Were the dogs in the house when you left last night?"

"Yeah, they were. I brought them in for her as I was leaving."

Thinking out loud the chief said, "They were outside when we got there this morning, on their chains."

The two men stood there, thinking about the potential ramifications of this new discovery.

"Would she have taken them back out, for being loud or something?"

"No, they don't make much noise once you tell them not to."

"I know. I've seen it. They're great dogs."

"Does anyone else know about 'Charlie'?"

"No, as I said, we kept that to ourselves. Even the boys don't know yet. Once everyone knows, their effectiveness as watchdogs goes away."

"Why Charlie?"

Williams thought for a minute then responded, "It's from Viet Nam. If the Charlies were coming we whispered 'Charlie' and everyone went quiet."

"Don't tell anyone else about it. Anyone. I'm not going to either."

"Okay, Chief."

Mason knew Williams would be true to his word. This was clearly a man who could keep a secret.

"By the way, your other dog is still up in Concord, at the PD up there. One of my guys is going to pick him up tomorrow."

"And my van?"

The chief paused, then keeping his cards close said, "It will probably be coming down tomorrow, too. If not, in the next few days."

With that, the chief knocked on the door and the officer outside let them out.

Chapter 20

Before he went home, the chief decided to go upstairs to his office one last time. He wanted to start the canvas of area bars and dance clubs right away, but he needed a picture of Mrs. Williams.

He called the officer down in the jail area and told him to ask Mr. Williams if he had a picture of his wife in his wallet, which was locked away with his other possessions. Williams did not.

The chief figured there must be a picture at the Williams' house, but he didn't want to send any of his men in without him there. He had stationed two officers there: one in his car in the driveway right beside the house and the other at the foot of the driveway. He instructed the men to patrol the area on foot every fifteen minutes. He hoped that would both keep his men awake and discourage any curious neighbors or local kids from snooping around the crime scene.

Mason gathered his things and left the station, taking the dogs with him. He decided he would pay a surprise visit to the officers. He had a lot of faith in Tim Wright, a relatively young officer, but had less confidence in Toyne, who was stationed by the house. The chief knew Toyne often slept through an hour or two of his night shift, but generally, there was so little going on that it didn't really matter. Tonight, though, he wanted everyone to be alert. The entire department had had a long day, and he knew they would all be tired.

On the way out of town, he stopped at the Burger King and picked up two large coffees. As he walked back to the car the labs had their heads poking out the half-opened windows, panting happily. The chief smiled, enjoying their company.

At about 10:15 PM, he pulled onto the Williams' street, the heavily wooded Milmar Court. The first one hundred yards of Milmar were relatively straight with three houses on each side. At the end of the straight portion the road doglegged to the right and went for another fifty yards or so before dead-ending into a circle. The Landers' house was at the end of the straight away on the left hand side. Then around the dogleg came the Williams' house and then the Bacons'.

The chief drove past Wright's car to turn in the circle and pull up behind him. Wright was alert as he pulled up and smiled and waved as he passed.

He debated letting the dogs out, but thought better of it. He grabbed the coffees and stepped out and walked towards Wright, who met him between the cars.

"Hey, Tim. Anything going on?"

"Hey, Chief. Yeah, there seems to be a pretty frequent stream of traffic. People from all over town seem to want a look."

Mason wasn't surprised. He knew from experience that people's morbid curiosity drew them to crime scenes. While he doubted that many would venture down the dark driveway even if he didn't have officers stationed there, he knew some would.

"I figured there would be. It should slow down in an hour or so, but you will still have to be alert. It's Saturday night and some of the local kids might think it's a good idea to try to sneak a peak or steal a souvenir."

He handed Wright the coffee.

"Thanks, Chief. The real action seems to be in back."

"What do you mean?"

"Well, about forty-five minutes ago, I saw lights in the house, so I ran back. It was Dave. He was walking around the yard and he thought he saw someone inside the house, so he went in to check. It turned out I saw his flashlight."

"And he didn't find anything?"

"No. Nothing."

"Okay, I'll go talk to him. Have you guys kept up the fifteen minute patrols?"

"Yeah. I just got back before you pulled up. Nothing's going on. Dave's been going pretty deep into the back woods. We figured if any kids did come it would be from that way, since they probably know we're positioned on the Milmar side."

"Good work, thanks. I'm going to go back and give this to Dave." He nodded towards the second cup of coffee and started to back to the house. "While I'm back there I'm going to go in the house for a few minutes, so if you see lights in there, don't be alarmed."

Toyne met him on the driveway, getting out of his car as Mason approached.

"Hey, Dave."

"Hi, Chief. What's up?"

"Nothing. I figured you've had a long, long day and could use this." He handed Toyne the second coffee. "Tim told me you saw something in the house?"

"Thanks, Chief, I can use it." He took the coffee and smiled. "Well, I thought I saw a light. I was on the other side of the house, on the Bacons' side, doing my check and I thought I saw a light move inside, like a flashlight. So I ran around to the side and went in. I figured it was probably a kid. I've heard noises out back in the woods, but I wanted to catch who ever it was so I went in." He pointed to the door by the family room.

"You went in through that door? Through the family room and the crime scene?"

Toyne could see the chief wasn't pleased.

"I know, but I wanted to catch him. I thought there was a chance it could have been the murderer, that is, if it's not Williams. And even if it wasn't, if it was just a kid, I didn't want him in there on my watch."

Mason tried to control his anger. Calmly, he asked, "Did you find anyone?"

"No, Chief, I'm sorry. I was sure I saw something, but maybe it was just Tim's light coming through the house. Anyway, while I was inside Tim saw my light and he came running. He opened the front door, announcing himself as an officer, doing everything by the book. I told him it was me. Then we checked the house together. But we didn't find anyone."

Mason patted the officer's back. "Okay, I can see why you went in, Dave. But you know you shouldn't have gone in alone. You should have had Tim watch the front while you watched the back and radioed it in. Then you should have gone in together, one in front and one in back, like we did this morning. You know procedure, Dave."

Toyne was a little surprised by how reasonable the chief was being. "Yeah Chief, I understand. I just wanted to hurry. But procedure is procedure. I'm sorry."

"Ok. It shouldn't be a problem."

"Thanks, Chief."

"Even so, you have had a really long day, Dave. As I was driving up I was thinking that I will send a second crew out to replace you and Tim at around midnight. You two can take station duty. When you get there, why don't you each try to get some shut-eye? Take two-hour shifts or something. You two work it out. Do you think you can handle another ninety minutes here?"

"Yeah, no problem. Thanks, Chief."

"Tim tells me there has been a fairly steady stream of people driving by out there." He pointed out to the street. "Aside from the light in the house, have you heard anything?"

The chief saw that Toyne's front car windows were each half open so that he could hear any noises.

"Yeah, I've been hearing sounds out back all night. Kids, I figure. I've been walking around a lot and turning my car lights on, just to make sure they know we're here."

"That's great. I think that should work." He pointed to the car windows. "I know it must be cold. The temperature has really dropped tonight. Good job on staying alert, Dave."

Toyne smiled, unaccustomed to praise from Mason. "Thanks, Chief."

Mason pointed towards the house. "I need to go inside for a minute."

"Why, Chief?"

"I need to find a picture of Mrs. Williams."

"What for?"

Mason didn't really want to go into Mrs. Williams' personal life, but the fact was he was going to have to explain to the officers who did the canvassing, so he might as well bring Toyne into the loop.

"Well, we just want to check around, see if Mrs. Williams has been seen in any bars in the area."

Toyne looked genuinely surprised. Mason figured that would be a pretty typical reaction among his officers.

"I thought you arrested Jim Williams, Chief. Do you suspect someone else?"

"I did. We did arrest him, but I just want to cover everything, Dave. You know how it goes."

The officer looked towards the house. "You want me to give you a hand?"

"No, you stay out here and keep an eye on things. The less we mess things up in there, the better off we are."

Toyne got the chief's not-too-subtle message. He looked down and replied, "Understood, Chief. Again I'm sorry."

"It's alright. It's just that this is the most serious case we've had around here in a long time and I want us all to do everything right."

Mason patted Toyne's back and headed to the front of the house, to the front door with his flashlight to guide him. The broken window was card-boarded over and there was a Harrison PD signed taped to the door, with "Crime Scene" written in bold marker. The door was closed and Mason knew the knob had already been dusted for prints. He turned the knob and went inside. Rather than turning on any lights, he used his flashlight to avoid touching anything he didn't have to.

The house was dark and a little bit stuffy. All of the windows had been closed to try to keep everything as stable as possible. He panned the light down the hallway towards the kitchen and then the family room. The blood splatters were not in his line of sight and things looked pretty normal. Mason considered how dramatically the lives of the people who lived here had changed since this time the night before. He traced the light back towards him, through the kitchen and into the front hallway.

There were some large-size family pictures on the hallway wall, but Mason hoped he could find something smaller and more focused on Susan's face. He carefully stepped to the right, trying to avoid the broken glass, and then walked into the wide entryway to the living room on the left.

The furnishings in the room were modest and old. He suspected that some were hand-me-downs from the Andersons. But the room looked happy. There were lots of family pictures, mostly of the boys and the dogs, but some with Jim and Susan, too. On a table by the front window he found a picture of Susan, a portrait from her college graduation. The picture was old, but she didn't appear to have changed too much. He compared it to a more recent picture, one of her and the two older boys. He was right. She hadn't changed much.

He checked around more and, finding no better alternative, kept the framed graduation picture and headed out.

As he stepped from the house he heard the dogs barking out front, he presumed from his truck. He had intended to talk with Toyne a little more, but he didn't want the Andersons and Williams boys to be disturbed by the barking so he hurried past him.

"Don't go back inside. Stay alert and I'll send out replacements for you guys in a little over an hour."

"Ok, Chief, see you later."

Mason hurried out to the street. Wright was standing near his car trying to calm the dogs.

"I'm sorry, Chief. A car drove around the circle and they went nuts. I've been trying to calm them."

"It's okay, Tim, I'll take care of them. Step back a bit so I can try to settle them down."

The dogs calmed a bit seeing him, but were still barking. With Wright out of range, he whispered quietly, "Easy, boys, easy. Charlie."

The dogs calmed down right away, but the chief cursed himself. He hoped the Williams boys hadn't heard the racket.

He walked back to an impressed Wright, but Mason was past accepting any more undue praise. He cut the officer off and said, "Dave explained what happened. You guys should have called it in before you went into the house."

Wright was a little taken aback, but knew the chief was right. "Yes, Chief. I know I should have."

"Okay, Tim. No problem. As I told Dave, I will be sending out replacements for you two at midnight. So you only have about an hour left. Stay alert, everything by the book."

Chapter 21

As he drove back to the station Mason tried to review his department's performance thus far. In his mind, they had made two big mistakes. The first was his own, not getting a picture out right away and starting the canvas of bars earlier in the evening. And the second was Toyne walking through the crime scene. He couldn't assess the impact of the first error, but felt that while Toyne's error was sloppy police work, it was not that big a deal.

Back at the station, he had copies of Mrs. Williams' portrait made and faxed out to nearby police departments. Then he instructed three officers to divide the region surrounding Harrison and canvas the bars and dance clubs in the area, starting in Harrison and working out from there. Additionally the officers would leave better quality copies of her picture at all of the local police departments so that they could conduct their own canvas as well.

Chapter 22

On Monday morning, Mason and the DA, Jerry Miller met in Mason's office to review where things stood.

"Anything new?"

"Yeah, quite a bit. But nothing conclusive either way, Jerry."

"Well, let's go through it."

"Okay, well, first off, I don't have the formal coroner's report back and I assume you don't either?"

Miller shook his head, confirming he didn't.

"Paul said he'll have more for me today. If there is anything there, I'll let you know. He did confirm that she was not raped and that there was no evidence of recent intercourse."

"I guess that doesn't help Jim Williams."

"I'm not sure. I guess not."

"What else?"

"Well Paul spent a lot of the time at the house on Sunday. He thinks the door to the boys' room was held shut. He can't prove that it was on Friday night, but there is evidence that at times a board was placed in between the door to the boys' room and the wall on the other side. The door opens out, so the board would make it impossible to open it."

"How did he figure that?"

"He noticed some paint chips on the carpet across the hall from the boys' room. When he checked more carefully, he noticed scratch marks on the floorboard, just above the carpet. He checked the other side and found similar scratches under the doorknob on the door to the boys' room. He figures a board was wedged between the door and the wall."

Thinking out loud, Miller added, "So the boys couldn't have gotten out if they were awake."

"Yeah, but it leaves a lot of questions."

"What do you mean?"

"Well, first, when was the board put there?"

Mason let that thought hang there for a minute then said, "Paul and I thought it through a couple of ways. On the one hand, let's say that Mrs. Williams, Susan had a lover. Then she might have been afraid of the boys coming out and finding her with him."

Miller nodded, waiting for Mason to go on.

"In some ways that makes sense in that it would explain how it could have been put there before she was murdered. But, the problem we have with that scenario is this: let's say she and her lover met there and they locked the boys in. That explains how the board got there, but it doesn't explain why it was removed."

"What do you mean?"

"Well, in that scenario we figured things started out well, well enough that maybe they were going to be intimate or be doing something she didn't want her children to know about. So she willingly blocked them in. Then some time later, things deteriorated to the point that she was murdered. After he killed her, why would the murderer have unblocked the door? The risk of the boys hearing him do it and coming out to identify him would just be too great. Why not just leave them locked in?"

Miller listened, nodding again.

"Maybe he would remove it to hide the fact that a person other than Jim and Susan had been there, but again that risks the kids coming out and catching him. The only other reason we could think of for removing it would be concern for the boys. That points to the father. Who else would take the risk?"

"So you think it was Jim?"

"I don't know. If it was Jim, why would he put it there in the first place?"

"If it was premeditated, he could have placed it there and then come back into the family room and killed her."

"I agree, Jerry. Paul and I discussed that, but nothing about this looks premeditated."

"I see what you mean, but he could have become enraged, blocked the door and then gone to kill her."

"Or it could have been the first scenario and the killer just took the risk, to hide his prints on the board or whatever."

"Did you find the board?"

"No."

"Then how do you know that paint chips weren't old? She wasn't the best housekeeper ever."

"You're right. She wasn't, but the scratches look fresh and the wood under the paint is still light. I'm not sure if Paul can pin down exactly when they were made. But, there is another scenario."

"Okay. Go ahead."

"When Ken Bacon went into the master bedroom to get the baby, he said he saw two wine glasses on the nightstand. When we checked, we found them in the sink in the kitchen."

"Any prints?"

"No, they were both wiped down."

"The way I see it, this confirms that the killer was there when Bacon took the boys out. As I mentioned the other day, when Ken first got there the side door was locked. He said he put his shoulder to it trying to open it. Fifteen or twenty minutes later when I went in that door, it was unlocked."

The normally unflappable Miller's eyes widened. "So the killer was in there when Ken went in."

The chief nodded. "He had to have been. Ken didn't see any car and the neighbors didn't notice any on Milmar. So he must have come in through the backwoods. Route 27 is only about three hundred yards through the woods out back and there are lots of secluded places to leave a car off 27. He could have easily parked back there."

"And walked right past the dogs?"

"They started the night inside. But in the morning he would have had to have passed them."

The DA just nodded.

"Yeah, that brings me to the third scenario."

Miller sort of rolled his eyes, not at Mason, but at the difficulty he knew he would have in proving any of these suppositions in court. "Go ahead, Matt."

"Let's say they, Susan and her lover, meet and get some wine, block the boys into their room and then go into the master bedroom. Then something happens, the baby starts crying, they have an argument, whatever. For whatever reason they leave the master bedroom and head back to the family room. Maybe at that point, if they're arguing, Susan just wants him out. She pulls out the board as she passes the boys room, or maybe runs into it."

"It's all just supposition, Matt. It doesn't get us anywhere."

"I know."

"So we're right back where we started?"

"No. We're not. Williams doesn't drink wine. Ken mentioned it, and Mr. Anderson confirmed it. He is a beer guy. Period."

"Oh, come on. Maybe he had one glass."

"His in-laws say he never does, ever. I'm not saying it's going to be good in court counselor. I'm just saying in my mind, there was someone else in that house that night and whoever it was must have been there in the morning. And that person was not Jim Williams."

"Why? Even if I buy that the wine glass wasn't his, Williams could have come home and found Susan and her lover." Thinking out loud Miller contradicted himself. "No, he would have killed them both or at least identified the lover. Or by now the lover probably would have come forward. But let's say Williams came home and noticed the wine glasses. That could have precipitated all of this."

"Then why would he wipe down the glasses?"

The two men sat quietly for a while, thinking.

Then Mason continued. "This gets even more difficult."

"Great."

"Yeah. Paul is pretty sure the time of death was between 11 PM and 1 AM. That's about as tight as he'll be able to get. So that means whoever did this either killed her and hung around until about 6:30 this morning or did it and left, then remembered the wine glasses and returned. When he came back he might have locked himself in. Then when he heard Ken, he panicked and ran when Ken went back to his house with the boys. In his panic, he forgot to lock the door."

"This is a mess. We don't have a clue as to what happened."

"Yeah, I know. But I don't think Jim Williams is our guy."

"And aside from your gut, your only real evidence is that you think he wouldn't have wiped down the wine glasses? And he wouldn't have because the prints wouldn't have been his because people say he doesn't drink wine?"

Mason rubbed his forehead. "Yeah."

"Did the canvassing yield anything?"

"Yes and no."

"That figures."

"She used to hang out at a bar up in Bloomsburg. The people there recognized her, and the cops did, too. One bartender said she liked to drink and pick up men. As good looking as she was, it couldn't have been too hard for her. Apparently they called Jim a couple of times when the owner said she was too drunk to drive home. But they said she hasn't been around for about a year and a half."

"How old is the baby?"

"About three months. It probably explains why they haven't seen her."

"And it begs the question of who the father is."

"Jeez, I hadn't thought of that."

After a minute Mason asked, "So what do you think, Jerry?"

"I don't know, Matt. Truthfully I'm not sure we have enough to hold Williams. Who does he have representing him?"

"Ted O'Hanlon. I imagine he's already got a call into your office."

"Well the Grand Jury convenes on Wednesday, let's try to put together our best case against Williams between now and then. I'm not saying don't continue to try to pursue other possibilities, let's just take our best shot at Williams."

Mason and Miller had worked together a lot over the years and Mason was familiar with this approach. They would pick their best candidate, try to build the best case against him or her, and then proceed on the evidence.

"Okay."

Chapter 23

During the next two days Mason and his department and Miller and his department built their case against Jim Williams.

While they did not want to ruin Mrs. Williams' name, they would if it became necessary. The fact that she had a history of seeing other men, a confirmed history, provided a motive for Jim Williams.

Their case, if they decided to take it to the grand jury, would be that Williams was the only one who could have killed her. He had the motive: jealousy. He had the opportunity: he lived there and arguably he alone could have kept the dogs quiet. Additionally, it could be argued that he was the only one who would potentially be willing to take the risk of removing the board that blocked the boys into their room. Finally, he had no alibi. By the time his van was discovered outside of Concord, he could have easily driven up from Harrison.

However, before they could convince a grand jury, they would have to get passed many facts that supported Williams' contention of innocence. Specifically, Williams clearly knew that his wife had been cheating on him for some time, at least since the time when Chief Mason brought her home two years earlier. So why after all this time did he suddenly snap on that Friday night? Next Mr. Bacon had seen two glasses of red wine in the master bedroom and those same glasses were subsequently found in the kitchen. Mr. Williams did not drink wine so who did the second glass belong to? And even if he did drink wine, given that it was his own house, why would he have risked coming back to the house to wipe the glasses down? As the husband and a resident, he could have easily explained them. Even if he returned to clear up other evidence against him, why would he have bothered with the wine glasses? Next the chief knew that anyone who knew the "Charlie" trick could calm the dogs, so when push came to shove, the dogs' silence was not really a viable argument that Williams was guilty. Next, if, as he contended, he left the night before at about 10 PM and didn't make any stops along the way, it is very plausible that no one saw him on his drive to Concord. If he left at 6:30 or so on Saturday morning, while it is still possible that no one saw him, it is less likely. Next, it could be argued that he of all people would have left the board on the door if he put it there, to protect his children from seeing their mother's body. And finally, his every action from the time he first met Officer Kipp suggested that he was completely shocked by what had happened. Examples of such actions include his giving his rifle to Kipp and the fact that his steering wheel and car had not been cleaned.

The truth was, while it was certainly possible that Williams killed his wife, there was also a reasonable doubt of his guilt.

In the end Miller and Mason decided not to go to the grand jury. If they were able to build a stronger case against Williams, they would indite him at some later date.

On Tuesday afternoon, having put off O'Hanlon for as long as they could, the DA and the Chief agreed they had to let him go.

Mason went down to the basement, to the cells. He instructed the officer on duty to open Mr. William's cell. Together they walked to the cell. Williams was standing, having heard Mason's instructions.

"Hi, Mr. Williams. Would you please come up to my office with me? If you have any personal things, please bring them with you." Williams picked up some reading glasses and a book from his bed.

The two men walked quietly up to Mason's office. Once inside Mason said, "Please sit down, Mr. Williams." Williams sat and the Chief settled behind his desk.

"You are being released, Jim."

Williams looked a little surprised.

"After we finish here, you can collect your wallet and other personal things and then we'll get you back to your kids."

"Okay, Chief. Good."

"The reason I want to talk to you . . . well, what you're going to face isn't going to be easy."

Williams looked at the chief. He respected Mason for the way he had handled the matter with his wife two years earlier and even for the way he had treated him since his wife's murder.

"What do you mean?"

"There are a lot of people in this town who think you killed your wife."

"I didn't."

Mason looked him in the eyes. He believed him, but did not want to say so. There were still too many questions.

"Truthfully, whether you did or did not doesn't really matter. Until and unless we find and convict whoever did kill Mrs. Williams, there are plenty of people who will think you did it."

He let that sink in. Williams didn't respond.

"Things could be really difficult for you here."

Finally Williams nodded.

"Have you thought about what you are going to do?"

He paused for a while and then said, "First, I want to see my children. Then I have to bury my wife. After that, I'll take things one day at a time."

Williams' only visitor in jail had been his lawyer. The fact that neither of his in-laws, his father-in-law in particular, had come to see him weighed heavily on Williams. He knew from the look Billy had given him on Saturday that he had to rebuild his connection with his oldest son, but he hoped he could do it with the support of Susan's parents. Now he doubted that he had that.

"Her body will be released from the coroner's office tomorrow."

"Okay."

They sat there awkwardly for a minute. The chief stood and said, "Come on, I'll drive you to the Bacons'."

As they walked out, Williams asked, "When can we move back into our house?"

"That's up to you. You will want to clean things up before you take the boys or the Andersons over there."

In his mind he still didn't know for sure if Williams had ever seen the murder scene or not. He decided to try a little test.

"Do you want to replace the carpet?"

Williams looked at him, confused and then surprised. With a little disappointment in his voice, he asked, "Do I need to?"

The chief immediately regretted his question, his cheap trick. Softly he said, "Yes, I think you will."

They drove in silence to the Bacons' house. Mason tried to win back Williams, to the extent he had ever had him, but Williams closed him out.

As they approached Milmar, Mason asked. "Should I bring the dogs over today?"

Williams thought about it for a minute and said, "I don't know. If we stay at the Bacons' tonight, if they let me, then I could keep the dogs at my house, outside. Can I go to my house if I want to?"

"Yes, sir. You are a free man, Mr. Williams. And your house is your house. I would ask that if you notice anything different once you are there, anything you think we might have missed, that you let me know."

Williams nodded.

"Were the dogs okay?"

Mason smiled. "They were great. My kids and I have wanted a dog for years, but my wife has resisted. We have just loved having them, Mr. Williams. They are the best behaved animals."

Williams almost smiled and said, "Thank you and thanks to you and your family for taking care of them. Please tell your wife how grateful I am."

"Honestly, it was our pleasure, even hers. I think she enjoyed them most of all."

It occurred to Mason that this may have been the first normal conversation Williams had had since Saturday. He thought, as he had a number of times over the past few days, that if Williams was innocent, he felt very sorry for him.

As they pulled onto Milmar Court he saw Williams eyes move towards the bend, towards his property. They drove slowly down the small street.

"I have had an officer stationed at your house since Saturday. I can leave him there for one more night if you like."

"Why?"

The chief hesitated. "I didn't want any prowlers or kids on your property. You know how people's curiosity sometimes gets the better of them."

"I just don't know. Can we leave it open until I find out where I am staying?"

"Sure, that's fine."

They drove past Williams' driveway and the chief turned into the Bacons'. "Listen, after you do this, when you go to your house . . . it's, well it's really bad over there. You may not want to see it. There are people we use to clean . . . to clean crime scenes. You don't want to do it yourself, Mr. Williams. Whether you choose to see it or not, you should have them clean it. They know how to really do it."

"Thank you."

Mason parked towards the front of Bacons' house. "Do you want me to go in there with you?"

He thought about it for a minute and then said, "No."

The chief looked across to him and reached out his hand. "Mr. Williams, I am sorry for your loss and for all that you have been through. If you need anything, please call me."

Williams shook his hand and said, "Thank you."

Then he stepped from the car and walked to the front door, more alone than anyone Mason had ever seen.

Chapter 24

Williams walked up two the steps to the Bacons' front stoop. He couldn't remember being so afraid in his entire life. He pushed the doorbell. He wasn't really paying attention, but he didn't think he heard anything. He waited for a minute and then pushed it again. This time he was sure he heard nothing.

He made a loose fist and knocked firmly on the door. Moments later he heard footsteps walking inside. His mother-in-law Emily opened the door. She looked up at him with an expression of shock on her face. He tried to read the expression, unsure of whether he saw fear or hatred or just plain surprise.

She stood there staring at him and then pulled the door all the way open. She stepped forward and slid her arms under his, pulling him to her, burying her face in his shoulder. He tentatively closed his arms around her. She hugged him tight. He felt her shaking against him, sobbing. He closed his eyes and hugged her back.

They stood like that for a while as she tried to compose herself. Then she pulled back a bit from him and looked up to him. "I'm so glad you're back. Frank and I both are. We need you here. The boys need you."

He couldn't speak at first. He had been so afraid that they too would believe he was guilty. Williams and his father-in-law got along fine, but his mother-in-law was one of his favorite people. She was extremely close to her daughter, her only child and knew that Jim was good for her, that he truly loved her. If she didn't believe in him, if she suspected him, he just didn't know what he would do.

She took a well-used Kleenex from the sleeve of her sweater and wiped her nose and eyes, trying to compose herself and fix her appearance. Then she took his elbow and led him down the hallway.

As they walked towards the family room his heart was racing. For days he had been picturing the look in Billy's eyes when he saw him on Saturday afternoon. He didn't know if he could bare it again. As the sound of their footsteps in the kitchen reached the boys and their grandfather, all three looked up from the card table in the Bacons' family room.

Williams was watching Billy. His first reaction at seeing his dad was one of happiness. He smiled for a second, his normal, past reaction. Then he seemed to catch himself and the smile faded. When Mike saw his father he jumped from the table and ran to him. Jim squatted as he leapt into his arms, then stood, holding him tight, the boy's feet dangling, wiggling happily.

Frank rose and smiled a small smile. He put his hand on Billy's back and nudged him towards his father.

Jim smiled and extended his right hand to Frank as he held Mike to him with his left.

Frank took his hand in both of his and said, "I'm glad you're back Jim."

"Thank you."

He released the grip and again squatted, still holding Mike. He put his arm around Billy and pulled him in, hugging him tight. His son didn't resist, but he didn't respond, either.

Williams just squatted there, hugging them. He couldn't imagine how they must feel. While he and their mom fought a lot, generally as a family they had had fun and been very happy. Now with their mother gone, and for the past four days their father gone too, they must have felt abandoned.

Jim looked up to his in-laws and said, "Thank you. Thank you both so much."

Emily was crying again and Frank moved to comfort her. Jim stood, his hands still on his sons' shoulders, holding them to him. He looked towards the baby Andrew, who was in a baby seat, playing with toys on his tray. Still holding Billy and Mike to his legs, Jim walked over and picked him up, hugging him, too.

Emily composed herself and said, "Who's hungry? Jim, you must be famished."

He smiled at her and responded, "I am."

She motioned for them to all sit at the kitchen table. While she made sandwiches and drinks for everyone, Mike chatted away, telling Jim what they had been doing with their grandparents, what fun they had had. While Billy was quiet, Mike's familiar chatter put Jim at ease.

Charlie

They ate and talked and ate more. The boys asked about the dogs and Mike about their things. It was clear he didn't understand why he couldn't go home. Jim hoped that meant that it was true that he had not seen the body. They talked about everything except their mother.

When it was finally bedtime for the boys, Mike showed Jim the room where they were staying. It had been the Bacons' son's room. While the boys were changing into their pajamas, Jim noticed a copy of *The Yearling* on the nightstand between the beds. It was a new copy, not the one from the library that he had been reading to them.

Once the boys were in the room's twin beds Jim sat down on Mike's bed and reached for *The Yearling*.

"Not that one Daddy. Grandma finished it." He handed his father the next book *Treasure Island*.

Billy, who had been quiet up until now, said, "Do we have to read tonight?"

"Yes, yes! Come on Daddy, please read it!"

Williams started to read and as he did Billy turned his back to them and pulled his blanket up tight, trying to ignore them.

After he finished, he had the boys say their prayers then kissed them goodnight and headed out into the family room.

Frank and Emily both rose from the couch as he walked back to meet them. He motioned for them to sit and settled into the comfortable chair across from the couch.

Jim began, "Thank you both for taking care of the boys."

"Of course, what else would we do?" Emily responded.

He could tell they had a lot of questions so he just let them control things.

His father-in-law looked to Emily and then started, "What do you think happened, Jim?"

He looked him straight in the eye and said, "I don't know. I just don't know."

Frank waited and then, seeing his son-in-law was finished, said, "Emily and I never believed, not for a minute that you . . ." His voice trailed off.

As Frank spoke, he was unsure if he was telling the truth. The first night, after they had put the boys to bed and had gone to bed themselves, he and Emily had hardly spoken. They couldn't.

But two nights later, on Monday night, as they lay in bed they finally did talk. Ted O'Hanlon, Jim's lawyer, told them that he felt Jim would not be indicted. He felt there was a good chance that he would be released without even going to a grand jury. So Emily and Frank talked. They could hardly comprehend that Susan was gone, let alone that someone had killed her. But they decided that if Jim was set free, they had to simply believe that he was innocent. He was going to raise their grandchildren. They could not live with doubt. They had to believe. And knowing him to the extent they did, they could believe. He was a good man. He was quiet and seemed aloof, but he loved their daughter and their grandchildren with all of his heart.

They knew too that their daughter was not a saint. Before she married Jim she had had some problems drinking, some drugs, going out with men. More than once, Frank had gotten calls late at night and had gone to pick her up at a bar or hotel. They had hoped that sort of behavior had stopped once she married Jim, but they weren't sure it had.

But in bed that night they decided he was innocent. For them it was simply a fact. Whether they could truly live with the decision, they did not know, but they wanted to.

After a long pause, Frank went on, "The police and the DA have questioned us and the Bacons. They said you two were fighting that night, Friday night. Were you?"

"Yes, we were."

"About what?"

He lowered his gaze. He did not want to discuss this, but they deserved it. He needed for them to believe in him. "We argued about money."

"You know you can always borrow from us, Jim."

"We're fine, I'm . . ." He stopped.

"So you fought and then left?"

He thought about it. "No. After we fought I put the boys to bed. Then did some chores around here. You know Susan, she would argue, but never stay mad. I left to go hunting at about ten, by then the argument was behind us."

"What happened next?"

"Nothing. At about noon on Saturday I came across a police officer in the woods. It turned out he was looking for me."

The three of them sat there for a few moments. Then Frank said. "Is there anyone you know who could have done this?"

"No. I just have no idea. I really don't."

For now, they left it there. They went through the painful process of discussing her funeral, deciding on a small private service with only immediate family. Afterwards they figured they would meet at the Bacons' and have as small a reception as they could, with the Bacons and a few of Susan's friends.

Emily made up the couch in the family room for Jim and she and Frank went to bed.

Jim considered going over to his house, but he decided to wait until the morning. He realized he hadn't called Mason. Hopefully he didn't mind keeping the dogs for one more night.

Chapter 25

The next morning everyone but Frank was up by seven. While Emily made breakfast, Jim found Ken Bacon's toolbox and with Mike's help, he opened up the casing surrounding the Bacon's doorbell, to figure out why it wouldn't ring.

Normally, Billy would have been the one helping him. Like his father, he loved building and fixing things. Billy was always getting into his dad's tools.

Jim found a disconnected wire and he showed Mike how to reconnect it. Then he had him press the doorbell. Mike was thrilled to hear it ring and pushed it over and over again.

If only to stop him, Jim helped Mike screw the doorbell casing back to the doorframe.

This is what he knew he had to do, try to get the boys lives back to normal as quickly as he could.

Frank came out of the Bacon's master bedroom, still in his pajamas.

Looking at Mike, he said, "Who's making all of this racket?"

Mike saw the smile on his grandpa's face and started to push the doorbell again. "Look, Grandpa, we fixed it!"

Frank took Mike's hand in his and smiled, "Good job, Mike. Come on, let's see what Grandma's cooking. It sure smells good."

As he led the boy back to the kitchen, he smiled at his son-in-law. The Bacons' generosity during all of this had been incredible and Frank was glad to see Jim doing little things for them. He knew that Jim would never mention it. He smiled, imagining that at some point the Bacons' would be shocked to hear their doorbell ring. They would be bewildered and answer the door, and then eventually realize that it must have been Jim who fixed it.

Frank had also been the beneficiary of his son-in-law's quiet repairs. On their last visit to Philadelphia while Frank had been golfing and Emily and

Charlie

Susan and the boys had been out shopping, Jim had fixed the Andersons' electric garage door. A few days after they had left, Frank was driving his car and noticed the garage door opener was on the sun visor. The last time he seen the opener, it had been in a drawer of his workbench in the basement. When he got home he pushed the button and watched with a smile as the door opened, knowing exactly who had fixed it.

"Mike, don't tell the Bacons' about the doorbell. It's more fun if they discover it themselves."

The boy's face showed his disappointment. In the past his father had said the same thing to him when he had fixed things. He said with a sigh, "Yeah, I know, Grandpa."

After breakfast, Jim called Chief Mason and apologized for not having called about the dogs the night before. The chief assured him that it wasn't a problem and that they would be happy to keep the dogs for a while longer if that would make things easier at the Bacons. Williams thanked him and said he was going to go over to his own house, to take a look. Mason told him he would radio the officer stationed there to expect him.

A few minutes later Williams went to his house, using the back way through the woods to avoid having to deal with his neighbors. As he approached, his heart raced. He purposely made a wide swing around the back of the house, partly to not startle the officer parked in his driveway and partly to avoid seeing inside.

He walked across the grass to the dirt area where the dogs were normally chained. As he did he saw the officer step from his car and come back to greet him. He didn't recognize the young officer and was unsure of the reception he might get.

"Hello, Mr. Williams. I'm Officer O'Donnell, Sean O'Donnell. The chief just radioed and said you might be coming over."

Williams was surprised as the young officer extended his hand. He took it and shook.

"Hi. Nice to meet you."

They looked at the house.

"Do you want to go in here or through the front, sir?"

Williams looked at him uncertainly and nodded to the side door, fifteen feet from them.

"It's locked, sir. Do you want me to open it for you?"

"Yes, please."

Williams followed him from the driveway to the door. He did not look through the window while O'Donnell unlocked it.

"Do you want me to go in with you?"

Williams looked at him and nodded. He opened the door and stepped in. Williams hesitated and followed, looking at his feet as he stepped in.

He looked up past O'Donnell. His eyes were immediately drawn to a huge dark stain on the carpet right in front of them. He followed the spot, which thinned to splatters and lead to a second spot, not as big as the first, but still big.

He just stood there staring.

After a minute, O'Donnell said, "I'm sorry, Mr. Williams."

Williams' eyes moved from the stains to the young officer. He didn't respond. He just stood there. After about twenty seconds, he turned and slowly walked out of the house, towards the police car.

O'Donnell followed him, leaving the door ajar.

With his back to the officer Williams simply, quietly said, "Thank you." Then he walked back into his backyard and over to the Bacons'.

Chapter 26

Frank and Emily saw Jim coming from his house, surprised that he was already on his way back. Emily stayed inside and Frank went out to meet him.

Jim approached, his face pale, his eyes lowered.

"That was fast."

Williams looked up at his father-in-law. He didn't want to tell him how bad it was. Instead he just looked back down.

Anderson seemed to understand. He lowered his head and gently rubbed his temples.

After a minute or so Williams said. "I need to talk to Chief Mason and then go to the funeral home."

"I'll go with you, if it's alright. I need to get out of here."

Williams considered what they would be doing, especially the funeral home part. While he could use his father-in-law's help with making decisions, he did not want to put him through that pain.

"You don't have to do this, Frank. I will take care of it."

"I know. Let me come, Jim."

Williams nodded. "I guess we better take your car. They still have my van and I don't want . . ." His voice trailed off. He didn't want to finish his thought out loud.

"That's fine."

"We may need to bring the dogs back, although I'm hoping Chief Mason won't mind keeping them for another day or two."

Anderson sort of smiled, knowing that Emily wasn't too fond of the dogs. "It would be easier if we don't have to bring them back, but if we do they can get in the backseat. It's not a problem."

After telling Emily what they were up to, Anderson and Williams drove into town. As they drove down Milmar one neighbor, Jeff Growley, was at the foot of his driveway, picking up his newspaper. As the car passed he looked up and was clearly surprised to see Williams, who was sitting in the passenger seat, looking out at him. Williams nodded a greeting while Growley just stared.

The men were quiet on the way to town. Jim was glad to be in his father-in-law's car, to be a passenger. They pulled into the police station parking lot and walked inside.

Even though Williams had spent the past four days there, everyone they saw and passed seemed to stop and stare.

He asked to see Chief Mason and they were led back to his office.

The Chief met them in the entryway and shook hands with both of them. Anderson was a little surprised, pleasantly surprised by the way Mason treated his son-in-law. He had seen the neighbor's look and the looks that the people here had given Jim. Mason on the other hand was treating him kindly, like a victim's spouse rather than a criminal. Anderson figured no one knew more about the circumstances of his daughter's death than Mason, and if he thought Jim was innocent, well, it was reaffirming for the father. He knew he would remember to tell Emily as well, to reassure her.

They went into the chief's office and discussed the case. Mason said they were looking in every direction they could think of, but had no new news.

After a while Jim asked his father-in-law if he would mind giving him a moment alone with the chief.

"Jim, I need to know everything. Please I'd like to stay."

"It's not about the case, Frank."

"What then?"

Jim didn't want to do anything to leave his father-in-law feeling he was hiding something from him. He was grateful that he and Emily seemed to believe in his innocence and did not want to do anything to change that. But he also didn't want to hurt him unnecessarily.

"I wanted to talk to Chief Mason about our house, about, um, about getting someone to clean it."

Frank nodded. He had walked towards his daughter's home several times over the weekend, wanting to try to piece everything together in his mind, but each time he had turned around, not wanting to really see.

He stood to leave. "Chief Mason, thank you."

Mason stood and shook his hand. He was surprised and glad to see Anderson with his son-in-law, for Williams' sake, for the Andersons' sake and even for his own sake. They seemed to believe in his innocence as well.

Charlie

"If there is anything I can do Mr. Anderson, please just call."

Frank nodded and stepped outside.

"Your father-in-law is a strong man."

They both looked at him, through the glass in the chief's door.

"Yeah. Susan was their only child. This must be killing him and Emily." Williams looked away, composing himself.

"I heard you went to the house."

"Yeah, I couldn't really go in passed the side door. I don't want to."

"I understand." Trying to make things easier for Williams, Mason asked, "Do you want me to have the people we use clean the place?"

"Yeah, please. The carpet, it is going to have to go, too. My kids can't ever see that." He paused, realizing as they both did that Billy had seen it. "And Billy can't ever see it again. They have to get everything. Everything."

"They will."

"I don't know how to do this, how much it's going to cost."

"I'll call them and have them go in and clean it, take out the carpet." He looked at his watch. It was 9:15. "I will try to get them in today. While they clean everything and take out the carpet maybe you can go pick new carpet, so you can control the cost. As far as the cleaners go, I imagine it will be $200 to $300, but I'm just guessing."

"Okay. Should I call them?"

"No, I will. Since it was a crime scene they will want it to be cleared by me."

"Thank you."

They started to head out of the office, opening the door. "Oh the dogs." Mason smiled. "You know who likes them the most?"

For the first time in days, Williams felt himself almost laugh. "Not your wife?"

Mason did laugh and everyone in the station noticed it. "Yeah. She won't admit it, but she loves them. Especially Brandy. We all love them."

"Would you mind one more day?"

"Mr. Williams, it's going to be so hard to give them back to you. We will keep them for as long as you want."

Chapter 27

Two days later they buried Susan. Only the Andersons, the Williams and the Andersons' minister were at the funeral.

Williams had been seen around town a couple of times, always in the company of his father-in-law. Anderson's presence with him helped to reduce the public presumption of Williams' guilt, but for most it just made the conversation more interesting. The consensus was that he was guilty, but that it couldn't yet be proved.

The day after the funeral the Williams and the Andersons moved back into their home. There was new carpet in the family room and the house was clean, very clean. Emily Anderson spent her first two days in the house changing sheets, doing laundry and doing more cleaning. She did everything she could to keep herself busy. She and Frank both dreaded the thought of going home, but they knew they would have to soon.

For Mike and Andrew, the move home was relatively easy. While Mike missed his mother, his grandmother and Aunt Helen doted on him and his brothers, and he seemed to be okay.

Billy was a different story. Everyone was nervous about bringing him home. When they first did, they all entered through the front door. Billy didn't even look down the hallway. He went into his bedroom and stayed there for as long as he could.

Eventually they drew him out for lunch. He walked warily into the kitchen and sat at the table, next to his grandpa. During the course of the meal he stole glances down to the family room and seemed relieved to see the new carpet.

They hoped that getting him back to school and into a more normal routine would help.

Charlie

From Jim's perspective being at home and seeing the work that Emily did made him acutely aware of how difficult his situation was. Assuming that he could find work, he would have to find someone to watch the boys and find the money to pay her. From the looks he had been getting during his trips into town with his father-in-law, Jim realized that Chief Mason had been right; many people did think he had killed his wife. He suspected that the handyman work he did around town would dry up. Already two jobs he had scheduled had called and cancelled.

A friend from the army, Jeff Griesch, owned a plant in Greenville, about twenty miles from Harrison. Griesch's company, Square Box, manufactured electrical boxes and employed about two hundred people. Williams hoped he could work there, but even if he could, it would be a time consuming commute. While Helen Bacon had offered her services, Jim knew she couldn't handle the long day that he and the boys would need. So he had to find work and he had to find someone to watch his boys.

Griesch had sent him a kind letter after Susan's murder and had written that if there was anything he could do, all Jim had to do was ask. Putting his pride aside, Williams decided to call him.

"Jeff, it's Jim Williams."

"Jim, it's good to hear from you." His voice softened. "I was so sorry to hear about Susan. How are you holding up? How are your kids?"

"Thanks, Jeff. We're doing okay."

Griesch wanted to ask about the case, but he was too good a friend to do it. They had been through a lot together in Viet Nam, and it never occurred to Griesch that his friend could be guilty.

After a short silence, Griesch said, "Jim, I meant it when I said if there is anything I can do for you, I want to."

"Well, yeah. I could use some help."

"Name it."

"I need a job, Jeff. Not a gift, a job. You know me. I'll work hard. I can fix anything. Just tell me what to do."

Griesch cut him off. "When do you want to start?"

"You know why I'm asking? People around here don't want to give me work. Are you sure?"

"Shut up."

Jim was quiet for another moment then responded, "Thank you, Jeff. Really, but I want you to be sure."

"Shut up."

Williams laughed into the phone. "How about Monday, boss?"

"Don't be late, Sergeant."

"Yes, sir, Lieutenant."

"I'll see you Monday. Just come to my office and we'll get you set up."

He was grateful to his friend. He had always known he could work for him at the plant, but never wanted to because of the commute and because he thought the work itself would be so tedious. But now, he knew he was lucky to get the job. He hoped the kindness would never be something his new boss would regret. Williams, who had worked hard at every job he had ever had, committed in his mind to being the best employee at the plant.

Now he had to find some one to watch the kids. His mother-in-law was going to stay on until he found someone, and Helen Bacon wanted to continue to help, but he needed to find a full-time sitter. It occurred to him that he had no idea what his new job paid. He'd have to find that out before he could figure out what he could afford to pay a sitter.

That night he went in to read to Billy and Mike. Billy still hardly spoke to him. He had to find a way to reconnect. He hoped that by resuming normal activities, things they had regularly done together that Billy especially liked, he would slowly bring the boy back.

He walked into the their room. They were both in their pajamas, playing rug hockey on the floor.

Mike looked up at him and smiled and then looked to Billy, "Next goal wins."

"It's ten-two Mike."

"So, next goal wins."

"Fine."

The boys took their shots until eventually the inevitable happened, Billy scored.

Jim was glad to watch them like this, just playing. "Okay boys, go brush your teeth then we'll read the next chapter."

Not looking at him, Billy said, "I don't want to read tonight."

Mike chimed in, "Well I do."

"So do I. You two go brush."

When they returned, Jim sat opposite them at one of the desk chairs. As he read, Mike listened, watching from the top bunk, but Billy faced the wall and pretended to be asleep. After he finished the chapter, he had the boys say their prayers and then kissed them each goodnight.

Charlie

He walked into the kitchen and sat with his in-laws. Except when they were with the boys, they avoided the family room.

"I have some good news. I got a job, a full time job in Greenville, working at a plant. A friend from the army owns it."

Frank smiled, knowing what a proud man his son-in-law was and what a relief that must be for him to find work. Emily smiled too, but added, "That's great, Jim. How far away is Greenville? What will you be doing?"

"Greenville is about twenty miles. It's about a thirty-minute drive. And the truth is, I don't know exactly what I'll be doing. My friend, the owner, is a guy named Jeff Griesch, I think you may have met him once in Philadelphia."

They both nodded, remembering him fondly.

"If you remember him, you might remember how he is. He is such a good guy. When I asked him for a job he just told me to show up Monday. I was so grateful I forgot to ask what I would be doing or what I would be paid."

The three of them laughed, but Jim could tell they had something on their minds.

"I imagine I'll be working on an assembly line. Once I sort it out and figure out how much I am making, I'll try to find a sitter for the kids. Would you mind staying for another week or two, Emily?"

She cut him off. "Don't be silly, of course. As long as it takes."

"Actually I think it might be easier, again if you don't mind, if you would help me interview the sitters, assuming we can find any."

They both understood. Most people in Harrison were treating him like a pariah. Frank spoke up, beginning cautiously.

"Jim, I have seen how hard it is for you here, how people treat you."

Williams looked down, embarrassed by the content and for his father-in-law having to have this awkward conversation.

"It will pass."

"I don't know. Don't you think it might be easier to move away? To Greenville, if you like the job, or to Philadelphia?"

He saw Emily's eyes light up. Clearly they had discussed this.

Jim was quiet for a minute then said, "I know it is going to be hard here at first, maybe always for me. But if I move, what message am I sending to the boys?"

"They're so young. Say for example you moved to Greenville or out by us. You are doing it to be closer to your work. You aren't running away from anything. You could just tell them that."

"They've been through so much, I don't know if another change is a good idea or a bad one."

With her back to the family room, Emily added, "Maybe it would be better not to be here, in this house, for Billy."

Williams thought about that for a minute, looking toward the family room. "You might be right, Emily. I don't know."

Until now Williams had thought he should deal with the way people were treating him the way he did most things, with his head up, moving forward. But if his in-laws couldn't stand to be in that room, how could Billy? Maybe he should move.

"Why don't we take things one step at a time? I'll go to work on Monday and see what that's like. If I feel as though it is stable and something I might be able to build a life for us around, then maybe we should move, at least to a different house."

They both smiled, noting that he had not said Philadelphia, but glad that he was being flexible, seeming to put the boys' best interest first.

Chapter 28

Chief Mason was getting frustrated with the investigation, as was the DA, Jerry Miller. The public opinion was that Williams had killed his wife. Word of the blocked door had somehow leaked and the citizen sleuths were all sure that he was the only one who would have done it and who could have quieted the dogs.

But the chief thought differently. He still worked to prove that Williams was the killer, but he was convinced it was another man, some very wrong man that Susan had become involved with. So he worked harder to try to find that man.

The police canvassing of bars outside of Harrison had been somewhat fruitful. A number of bartenders and bouncers remembered Susan, though most said they hadn't seen her in a year or two. There was one bar in particular that she seemed to have especially liked. It was in Bloomsburg, a town about thirty minutes west of Harrison. The place, Al and Larry's, was sort of a dive, a big dance bar with live music several nights a week. Apparently, for a while at least, she had been a semi-regular there.

Mason drove to Bloomsburg and talked to both the local police and to the people at Al and Larry's. Most of the waitresses and bartenders there were pretty transient, but there were a few who had been around for several years and remembered her, especially one bartender. He said that on quiet nights she would sometimes sit and talk to him. He was married too and so far as Mason could tell, just a nice, decent guy.

The bartender remembered that towards the end she mostly seemed to meet one guy there, though at times she would be game for other men. He said that one night her sort of regular guy had shown up and he had found her with another man she had just picked up. Apparently the regular guy went nuts, yelling at her and the poor other man she was with. But the bartender didn't know the regular guy and couldn't describe him other than to say that he was white, mid-thirties and thin, about average height.

Since then the chief and the Bloomsburg police had tried to gather more information about the guy, but had come up with nothing. No one at the bar remembered what kind of car he drove or even what he did. He wasn't a local. In fact, they sort of had the sense that he was from wherever she was from, though they never arrived together. They checked the local motels and also motels between Bloomsburg and Harrison, but those inquiries all came up blank.

So Mason was unable to really find another man and likewise he hadn't made any progress in proving that Williams was guilty or innocent. The more time that passed, the deader the case became. At this stage, Mason felt that the best if not only hope he had was that the killer would make a mistake.

Chapter 29

Williams started his new job and liked it. At first people treated him with some distance, clearly the rumors had made their way to Greenville, but they came to respect his hard work ethic and his ability to fix anything.

The pay was good, too. He was making more than he had in the past and now had medical benefits. However, while his work situation was good, things at home were not. Emily had found him a daytime sitter, but she wasn't working out. With the boys she was a mean, lazy older woman. Helen Bacon kept a sharp eye on her and, Jim suspected, probably did a lot of the cleaning work that the lady was supposed to do. On top of that the house itself was just too painful for Billy and for his in-laws when they visited. He had to move.

Really the only downside of moving would be losing Helen Bacon. But Jim knew that he was taking advantage of her as it was.

The more he thought about it the more he needed to get the boys out of there, especially for Billy's sake.

He talked to Griesch about both his housing situation and to ask him if he or his wife knew of any one who might want a job sitting for the boys.

The housing issue turned out to be easy. Griesch had suggested that he move to Greenville, but if he could Williams wanted to stay in Harrison to keep his boys in the same schools. While he was being treated poorly or at least with distance, people generally treated his sons with compassion. He did look for a new house in Greenville, but ended up finding one in Harrison, albeit one that needed a lot of work. In addition to being bigger than his current house, the new house was on the other side of Harrison and took about ten minutes off each leg of his daily commute. While Jim knew he would take a hit on his current house, because of its history, he still thought he could sell it. He kept it in such perfect condition that any future owner would be in good shape in terms of repairs and things for some time. If he could sell his current house, he would put a bid on the fixer-upper.

A week or so later, Griesch told him to come up to his office at lunchtime. At 12:30, his lunch break, he went into the office part of the plant. Jeff's secretary told him to go right into her boss' office.

He knocked on the open door and his boss waved him in. As he entered, a woman who looked to be in her late thirties turned to face him.

"Jim, this is Betsy Barrett, my accountant."

Williams smiled and stepped forward, shaking her hand. "Its nice to meet you."

She smiled. She was about thirty pounds overweight and plainly dressed, but she had a kind, pretty face.

"Hi, Mr. Williams. It's nice to meet you too."

Jeff pointed to the seat beside her and Williams sat.

"Jim, Betsy is my accountant, not the company's, mine. She does my taxes and lots of other people's around here. But really it's part time. She is interested in the job with your boys."

Williams was genuinely surprised. She looked more like an accountant or even a lawyer than a sitter. As he looked at her, they both apparently read his thoughts and laughed.

"Betsy used to sit for Amy and me, for our girls. She's great."

To William's further shock she started to try to sell herself. "I have lots of experience with kids, Mr. Williams. I don't have any of my own, but I just love kids. I babysit for everyone. Mr. Griesch has explained the situation. I can clean and cook, watch them. I have a car so I can do the grocery shopping and stuff."

Jim was surprised, a little overwhelmed. She seemed perfect. "I'm not sure how much I can pay Mrs. Barrett. I have a woman in Harrison now. I pay her about $175 a week."

"Whatever you think is best, Mr. Williams. If it is all right, I will do some of my tax work during the day when the older boys are at school. It provides a nice income for me, but during most of the year it doesn't take much time, and I would never put that work before the boys."

Jim looked at her. She seemed great, too good to be true. He looked at Griesch, who again seemed to read his thoughts.

"Jim, all I know is I asked Amy if she knew anyone who might want to the job of watching your kids and she immediately said Betsy. Then before I knew it Betsy was on the phone asking me about the job."

They both turned their eyes to her. She seemed embarrassed by the attention. Reluctantly she looked at them both, then focused in on Williams.

"Amy told me about your situation, Mr. Williams. I am so sorry for your loss."

Jim was moved by her kindness. She seemed to have taken Amy at her word. Aside from Griesch, his in-laws and the Bacons, few people had been that kind to him since that day.

He looked at her again. She seemed sincere. "Do you know everything? About the rumors?"

"Mrs. Griesch, Amy told me everything and she told me what you did for Mr. Griesch in Viet Nam. I can help you Mr. Williams and it's what I want. I'm forty-two years old. I'm Miss Barrett, Betsy, not Mrs. Barrett. I don't have any children of my own and I love kids. Your poor boys have been through so much. Please give me a chance."

He smiled at her. "Well, Miss Barrett, you seem perfect to me. I am in the process of moving, at least trying to move. We're in Harrison. But as soon as I can sell the house we're in now I want to move to a new house, still in Harrison, but closer to here. I have an older woman watching the boys now, but she is not working out."

He paused for a minute. "Would you mind talking with my mother-in-law? She is much better at this sort of thing than I am, and she wants to help. Would you mind talking to her?"

"Of course not. I'd love to meet her."

Chapter 30

About two months later the William's moved into their new house in Harrison. Because of its history their old house on Milmar had sold for about 35% less than any other house on the street, even though they were all essentially the same and no house or property was better maintained than the Williams'.

But the new house was perfect. It had four bedrooms, two for the three boys, one for him and a guest room for his in-laws. Jim wanted their influence on his boys and wanted to make the Andersons as comfortable as he could.

The house needed a ton of work and because of that he had been able to afford it. But he liked the bones and knew he could make it perfect. He also hoped that Billy would be happier there. Jim knew he was hurting badly.

A month or so before they were due to move in, Williams had asked his mother-in-law Emily to come down when she could to talk a woman he was thinking about hiring to take care of the boys. She and Frank were thrilled by the news that they were moving and that they were getting a new babysitter. Emily had hired the current sitter, but not by choice. She had been the only one she could find willing to work for Williams.

About a week later she and Frank drove down to see the boys and to see the new house. The previous owners had moved out of state and the house was empty. Jim arranged for the realtor to meet them and open the house.

They all met there, so the boys could see the house, too. It was in a development, on a series of manufactured streets built in the late sixties. There were four different types of houses in the development and the Williams' was one of those. It was a center hall colonial. Downstairs there was a living room, a den, a kitchen, a dining room and a powder room. Upstairs there were four bedrooms and two baths. And there was a basement.

Charlie

While the boys were excited by the size of the house and its great open yard, Frank and Emily were a little surprised by how beat up it was, especially inside.

Jim could see that they were too kind and polite to ever say anything so he helped them out once the boys were out of earshot.

"I know this place is a mess now, but the pipes are good, the appliances are good and it's soundly built. I'll have it fixed up in no time. If it wasn't such a mess, I wouldn't have been able to afford it."

They seemed relieved and tried to look at it from a different perspective. Jim walked them through his plans for fixing it up and asked for their input especially in terms of the colors he should paint certain rooms and how he might set up the furniture. Their outlook seemed to brighten.

"It's just so much work Jim. How are you going to get it all done?"

"Well, actually I was going to ask for your help with that."

They were both really taken aback by this. Their son-in-law was a proud man and rarely asked for their help. And in this instance, they thought their help might actually be more of a hindrance; they had neither the strength nor the skill to be of much use.

"Do you mean to help you clean it?"

He laughed. "No, of course not. I was wondering. Well, how would you feel about taking the boys to Philadelphia or to the Jersey Shore with you for a little vacation? The plant closes for the first two weeks of every July and I take possession here on June 27th. If you guys have the boys, I could just work fulltime on fixing it up."

Frank and Emily both burst out laughing. They had asked Jim if he and the boys or just the boys could come out and spend some time with them during the summer. With Jim's new job they didn't think he would be able to get away, but they hoped he would let them take the boys.

Frank let Emily do the talking. She looked at Jim and smiled, saying, "I think we would be willing to do that."

Jim thought it was the happiest he had seen them since their daughter's murder.

"Thank you." He looked at his watch. "Emily, we should get going. I want you to meet Miss Barrett. I figured it would be better if we met at a coffee shop. If she sees this place like this, she'll change her mind."

"Are we all going to meet her?"

"At first, yes. She is really nice. I want the boys to meet her. I want them to be excited about the new house and about her. And I think she should meet them too. But we'll just meet outside, and then you two can go in and talk. See what you think about her."

Chapter 31

Betsy Barrett walked nervously outside Lou's Diner on the main street of Harrison. Mr. Williams had asked her to meet him and the boys and his in-laws there at 1:30. She had already been there for twenty minutes and it was only 1:25.

She didn't know why she was so nervous. Her first meeting with Mr. Williams had gone really well and in their subsequent two phone conversations he had seemed very positive. Additionally, her inside source, Jeff Griesch's wife Amy, had told her that Jeff had said that Jim Williams had told him she seemed perfect.

That morning Betsy had been a wreck. She had changed her clothes about three times finally settling on a blue sundress that she hoped didn't emphasize how heavy she was getting.

On her fourth trip past the diner, she saw Mr. Williams approaching with two boys and an older man and woman pushing a stroller. They all looked happy. She gathered herself and walked towards them.

Williams smiled what seemed a genuine if shy smile when he saw her.

"Hi, Miss Barrett." He extended his hand.

"Hello, Mr. Williams. It's nice to see you again." They shook hands. Betsy was surprised by how rough his hand was.

"Miss Barrett, this is Emily and Frank Anderson. And these are my boys, Billy, Michael and Andrew."

Betsy shook hands with the Andersons and then with Billy and Michael. The boys were polite, but guarded.

"I understand you boys are moving into a new house."

They both responded simultaneously, "Yes, ma'am."

"Have you seen the house yet? Your new neighborhood?"

Mike spoke up. "Oh yes, we were just there. It's huge and we have a giant backyard."

Betsy smiled, drawn in by Mike's enthusiasm. "Did you meet any of the other kids, any of your neighbors? It's a great area. There are so many kids around there."

She looked up at Mr. Williams and the Andersons. "Mrs. Griesch told me about your new house."

Mike responded. "We saw some kids when we drove in, but we haven't met any yet."

She smiled looking straight at him and spoke in a soft, kind voice, "I'm sure you will, Michael. By the end of the summer, you'll have more new friends than you can imagine."

"Do you think so?"

She nodded reassuring him. "Oh yes. I'm sure." Then she turned to Billy. "And Billy, I understand you are going to turn twelve?"

"Yes, ma'am, next week." His tone was polite, but reserved.

"I heard that. I hope you don't mind, but I got you something." She opened her big leather purse and pulled out a small package and handed it to him. "It's nothing fancy, but I hope you like it, Billy."

He took the small package, surprised and smiled a bit. "Thank you, ma'am." He turned to his father. "Can I keep it?"

Williams smiled and nodded. "Sure, but you have to open it first."

After hearing Billy's immediate question Miss Barrett was afraid that she might have dome something Mr. William's found objectionable. She quickly added, "It's really just a small gift."

Williams looked to them both. "I'm sure it's fine. That was very nice of you Miss Barrett."

She was embarrassed, but knew the boys had been through so much and just wanted them to have a warm first impression of her. Reddening, she reached into her purse again and pulled out a second, smaller package and handed it too Michael.

She bent and turned to him. "I know it's not your birthday, but this is for you."

Michael took the present without hesitation. "Thank you, ma'am. May I open it?"

She and Michael both turned to face the boy's father.

"Go ahead, Mike."

He ripped open the tiny package.

"As I said guys, it's nothing fancy, just some little things I hoped you might enjoy."

Mike opened his and found a little plastic covered toy baseball field with four metal balls that the player tried to get into four holes where the bases were. Billy's was a metal and wood contraption, a mind puzzle.

They both seemed to enjoy the gifts and thanked her and started to try to play with them. She smiled her kind, infectious smile and turned to Andrew in his stroller. She reached into her purse and placed a tiny stuffed animal, a little orange duck, about four inches long, into his hand. She smiled at him too and then stood.

"That was awfully sweet of you, Miss Barrett."

"It's Betsy, Mrs. Anderson."

"It's Emily."

The four adults stood and talked for a minute or two while the boys tried to solve their puzzles. After a while Betsy and Emily went into the coffee shop while Frank and Jim and the boys explored town.

Chapter 32

By the time June 27th came, Williams had the house on Milmar mostly packed up and was ready to go. Until then he hadn't touched Susan's things. They were all still as she had left them in their bedroom and in the various closets and storage areas. Even as he packed he had decided to simply put her things into boxes and store them in the attic of the new house rather than dispose of them or give them away.

They had shared a large dresser in the master bedroom and four of the six drawers contained her things. Originally he had planned to just pull out the drawers and load them into the truck full. But he felt it might be better, for now at least, to pack them away. So he emptied her drawers and his. When he finished he looked at the big, now-empty dresser and doubted he would ever really fill it again.

On the morning of the move, as Williams and the independent mover he had hired were loading the truck, Chief Mason pulled into their driveway on Milmar. Williams had told the chief of his plans and the chief agreed he was probably doing the right thing. In fact Mason was surprised he wasn't moving out of Harrison altogether. While the uproar over the murder had died down over the subsequent months, the townspeople's feelings about Williams hadn't really changed and Mason doubted they would unless the true killer was found. And Mason knew too that he was one of the few who believed that the killer was not Jim Williams.

When the chief got out of his car the dogs ran to him and greeted him happily. Mason bent and patted them all.

As Williams approached him, Mason looked up and smiled. "You taking these guys with you?"

"Yeah, Chief. Sorry."

Mason laughed and stood up and shook his hand.

"You all packed?"

"Just about. Just some of the furniture left now. We packed most of the boxes and things last night."

Along with the dogs they walked up to the back of the open mid-sized moving van. Mason wasn't surprised to see how well organized the inside was.

"Well I hope it goes well for you in the new house. And for the boys."

"Thank you."

"And I want you to know, I am not quitting on trying to find out who did this."

Mason looked at Williams and then reluctantly pushed him one more time. "Look, Jim, I've always had the feeling that you were holding back on me, that you were protecting someone."

He looked around to be sure no one else was within earshot. "You may not want to hear this again, but as I've told you before it's pretty clear she was still going to Bloomsburg for quite a while after that time I drove her back here. And it seems as though for a while at least, she was just seeing one guy. Do you have any idea who he was?"

Williams looked right at him, his eyes revealing nothing. Over the months the two men had come to respect each other, but Williams had never opened up.

After a minute, he just shook his head.

The chief wanted to press him more, but he doubted it would do any good. He had the feeling he would never know who killed Susan Williams.

Chapter 33

The new house and the new arrangement with Betsy Barrett were working out well. Williams had been able to get the place into clean, workable shape while the boys were in Philadelphia and on the Jersey shore with their grandparents.

When the five of them came back to Harrison, they had all been thrilled with what he had done. Even Billy seemed pleased. His father had decided to give him his own room and had made it a surprise when they got back. Mike was disappointed to be away from his big brother, but Williams knew he would get over it quickly. Frank and Emily were pleased too. Jim had purchased used furniture for the guest room and made it clear that it was their room and that he wanted them to come as often and stay for as long as they wanted.

Betsy Barrett had been really helpful, too. She had shown up on Jim's third day of working on the house and had insisted on helping him with the cleaning. Additionally, with Jim's encouragement, she had helped him set up the boys' rooms and the other living areas. On her second day, she arrived with groceries and Jim quickly discovered that she was a good cook.

As they worked together and separately on setting up and cleaning the house, he was increasingly sure that he and his mother-in-law had made the right decision in hiring her. She was a secure and thoughtful person to be around. Additionally, she was comfortable with silence, as was he. And once the boys got home, they took right to her, even Billy. She was kind and fun loving, but demanded respect, too.

So they settled into a new routine. That first summer, before school started, Betsy would show up in the morning before Jim left for the plant. She would make them breakfast, tend to them while he worked and prepare dinner for when he arrived home. Some nights she would eat with them, but most nights she would not. On the rare nights when Jim had to work late at

Charlie

the plant, she would happily stay with the boys until he got home. Jim came to know that aside from her accounting work and her church, she did not have much of a life beyond her life with them. It was clear that what she had said that first day he had met her had been true; she did in fact love kids and she was a great help to them.

Jim's choice of neighborhood was working out well, too. The boys had quickly made friends with the many kids in the neighborhood and literally spent their days outside playing and exploring. But for Jim, things were different. Most people still believed that he might have killed his wife. As a result, while his kids were generally welcomed as innocent victims, Jim himself was treated with caution. He was acutely aware of the treatment and with his already introverted nature his life became increasingly isolated. He did interact with others at work and with his boys and Betsy at home, but beyond that he kept pretty much to himself. All of that took a toll on him. He was lonely and a little bitter and away from home and to an extent work, he viewed people with increasing cynicism.

At work, rather than being treated as a murderer, he was simply an employee and as time went on, an increasingly valued one.

Griesch ran the plant with non-union employees. While he was the company's owner, he made sure that everyone who worked there had a vested interest in being productive and efficient. Employees were paid on an hourly or salaried basis, depending on the skill level of their job, but at the end of each year, Griesch had set up a profit-sharing plan wherein he paid bonuses to each employee on the basis of the company's profits and more subjective views on individual contribution. He knew that he was in an increasingly competitive business and that if he had a motivated, well-compensated, lean work force, both he and his workers could benefit. He kept and paid employees who worked hard and got rid of those who did not. He insisted that supervisors and managers gave their workers regular performance reviews and rewarded employees at all levels for productivity enhancing ideas.

As a result Square Box workers generally appreciated hard work and consequently Williams fit in well there. About a month after he started, one of the conveyor belts that were the lifeblood of the manufacturing part of the plant broke down. The in-house electricians charged with keeping the belt running felt that the belt would have to be down for the better part of the day, which would reduce that day's output by about 40%. Jim quietly stepped forward and made a few suggestions for some temporary, makeshift repairs. The floor supervisor agreed with Jim's suggestions and helped him implement them. Twenty minutes later they had the belt up and running. Rather than taking credit, the supervisor told the plant manager that it was Williams who had come up with the solution. A week, later Jim found an extra $400 in his weekly paycheck. He quickly developed a reputation as a guy who could fix most things. When something mechanical or electrical went wrong, Jim would get taken off the line and brought in to help. The plant's chief engineer, Scott Oats, came to appreciate Jim's practical know-how and started to consult him on a variety of issues, from purchase decisions to maintenance plans and schedules.

So, for part of his day at least, Jim had found a place. He was making more money than he ever had before and actually liked going to the plant every day. Billy and Mike seemed to be happy with their new lives in their new neighborhood as well and with Betsy. But in spite of all that, Jim mourned the loss of Susan and felt as though he had lost his oldest son and all of that weighed heavily on him.

Before the school year started he decided to take Billy camping with him, just Billy, to try to bring him back. The Andersons came to stay with Mike and Andrew and on an August Friday, Williams and his oldest son headed off with the dogs. They had spent the prior week planning and Betsy, who was well aware of Billy's standoffishness with his father, had worked hard to build up the trip. Williams appreciated her enthusiasm but had to laugh at her idea of camping. By the time they left she had made so many brownies and sandwiches and coffee cakes, that they had enough food for a week. Williams was sort of a minimalist, but in this instance, while he did want to start to teach his son how to survive in the wilderness, he felt it was more important that they simply have a good time together. So he packed the large picnic hamper and cooler that Betsy had prepared into his van. He wasn't sure how he would get all of the supplies from the parking area to the spot where he planned to hike and then camp, a distance of about four miles, but he would figure something out.

As they headed out Williams wanted to break the frequent silence between him and his son right away. "Betsy sure has made us a lot of food."

The boy looked into the back of the van, at the hamper and cooler among the backpacks and camping gear. He responded nervously, "She sure did."

"I don't think we can carry it all with us, so we better try to eat some now. Why don't you get some of those brownies of hers and we can eat them on the way up?"

Charlie

Billy looked at him, surprised. Normally his father didn't eat sweets and discouraged his boys from eating them, too. He unfastened his seatbelt and tentatively made his way into the back of the van.

"Would you grab us two Pepsis, too? I think she put some in the cooler."

This really threw Billy. His father never drank soda. He rooted through the hamper and found the brownies and then took two cans of Pepsi from the cooler.

"What else does she have in the cooler?"

Billy took an inventory. "Let's see. There are eggs, bacon, milk, some hamburger meat, buns and little packets of ketchup and mustard."

"Eggs?"

Billy looked up to the front of the van. "Yes, sir, eggs."

"I don't think she has ever been camping. At least not really camping."

"What do you mean?"

Jim was already glad for the trip. This was the most he and his son had interacted in months. He and Betsy had had to force the boy to go and even now he seemed to be almost afraid. "Well tomorrow night we are going to camp at a spot I know. It's about four miles from where we will park the van. I had been planning to hike about a mile tonight, but maybe we should rethink that."

"What will we do instead?"

"I'm not sure. I see two possibilities. First, we could hike to the spot I originally had in mind. It's not an easy hike and between the tent and our backpacks and the other gear and the food we will need for tomorrow and Sunday, we wouldn't be able to bring much of Betsy's food with us."

Billy nodded, listening.

"Or we could camp at another spot I know. It's not as good as the spot I originally had in mind, but it's close to where I want to leave the van. If we park there we can go back and forth to the van. That way we can cook the burgers tonight and the bacon and eggs tomorrow morning. It's not exactly what I had in mind, but if we do it that way, we won't hurt Betsy's feelings and we can still rough it tomorrow night and Sunday. What do you think?"

The boy thought about it. He did want to rough it, but he knew how excited Betsy had been about preparing things for them. "Can we really still rough it tomorrow night?"

"Oh sure. There is a lake where we are camping tomorrow night. We can spend the day fishing and hunting by the lake. We'll eat what we get."

"And the place where we will camp tonight, it's not a parking lot or something?"

"Oh no, Billy. We will park at the end of a dirt road. There aren't usually even any other cars there. The spot I'm thinking about is only a few hundred yards into the woods from there, but it is in the middle of nowhere. It's a terrific spot, too."

"Then do you think we should do that? So that we don't hurt Betsy's feelings?"

"Ok. If it's ok with you, Billy, that sounds like a good plan to me."

As they drove along Williams told his son about camping, explaining things like ground sheets and rain flaps. Billy ate it all up and asked lots of questions. For the first time since Susan's death, he seemed like his old self.

About two hours later they reached the end of the dirt road and parked. Jim loaded Billy up and together with the dogs they headed to the spot where they would spend the night. On the first trip they had the tent and their backpacks and sleeping bags. The excitement Billy had shown in the car turned back to nervousness. Jim sensed his change of mood and tried to bring him back.

"Billy, we have two things we have to do before it gets dark. First we need to find firewood, lots of it. Then we need to set up the tent. Let's get the wood first."

They put the gear down and started to move around the area, panning out into widening circles. Together they gathered what seemed to Billy to be an awful lot of wood.

"Now we need to find a spot to set up the tent. Where do you think? We need a nice flat spot without a lot of roots or rocks sticking up from the ground. Otherwise sleeping will be really uncomfortable."

Billy looked around and picked what looked like a good spot to him. "How about here?"

"That's the spot I was thinking, too. Okay, let's put the tent up."

Jim helped Billy but had the boy do most of the actual work, so that he would learn how to do it. Once the tent was up they headed back to the van, to get the food and other supplies. Then Jim showed Billy how to start the fire, again having Billy actually do it. They soon had a good fire going and started to cook Betsy's burgers.

"Why don't you do the cooking?"

Billy kind of laughed. "You want me to cook?"

"Sure, you can do it. I'll walk you through it."

Charlie

"Okay."

The boy cooked the burgers and along with that they had potato salad that Betsy had made.

They sat on rocks and ate.

"Mmm, this is great. There is nothing better than campfire food. And your burgers are really good, Billy."

After dinner Jim took the cooler back to the van, leaving Billy and the dogs at the fire. It was a clear night and even though they had the tent set up, they decided to sleep outside, looking up at the stars.

While his dad was at the van, Billy was playing with a stick in the fire. He let the end catch and then waved it around like a sparkler. He stood and started to run around with it, waving it up and down, the red embers making light-streak letters. As he ran and waved it the top portion broke off and fell onto the tent as he passed. Billy didn't even notice. He just kept running around in circles with the dogs chasing him.

After a bit the embers on the stick died out and he sat back at the fire, playing with more sticks there.

His father returned, seeing Billy poking at the fire, as kids and adults are prone to do. He went to sit by Billy when he noticed a glowing spot on the tent's rain cover.

He yelled as he got back up. "Damn it Billy, what happened?"

Williams ran to the tent and put the calloused heels of his palms on either side of the rain cover, smothering the glowing edges of a hole burning into the nylon. Once he was sure that portion had stopped burning he looked inside, at the tent itself. A growing, glowing hole was burning it, too. To get to it Williams quickly pulled up the stakes of rain cover and reached inside and pulled down the tent's supports. Then he stomped on the flattened tent, again smothering the burning nylon. Once that portion was out he crawled into the partially collapsed tent and found a third hole smoldering in the tent's bottom. He ground his jean-covered knees against the burning area and again put it out.

During all of this Billy stood nearby, watching and waiting for his father to lay into him. When he was sure everything was out, Williams replaced the tent poles and stakes and tightened everything up, surveying the damage and triple checking that everything was out. He did all of this silently, trying to contain himself. Already he was regretting his initial outburst. He was trying to mend things with his son, not make them worse.

Kneeling in front of the tent, he looked at his son. He could see him slipping back away. He stood and walked over to him. The boy cowered. Williams' heart sank and he squatted, facing the boy.

"I'm sorry I yelled at you, Billy. Really I am."

Billy raised his eyes and looked at his father, surprised that he was apologizing instead of yelling.

His dad rose and started around to the other side of the tent. "Come here. I want to show you something."

The boy nervously followed him around. Away from the fire it was too dark to see so his dad grabbed a flashlight. He unfastened and lifted the rain cover and shined the flashlight on the side of the tent, panning over it, searching. Eventually the beam stopped on a nylon patch, sewn onto the tent.

"Do you see that patch?"

"Yes, sir."

"Any idea how that got there?"

"No, sir."

"That one was my fault. One night a few years ago I pitched the tent too close to the fire. I pitched it up wind, so that smoke and sparks and cinders would blow away from it, but the wind shifted and a big old cinder blew right into my tent. And look at the size of my hole, it's a lot bigger than yours."

Billy looked at the hole and then his father. His dad was smiling.

"Do you know how much it cost me to fix that hole?"

"No, sir."

"About two dollars, Billy."

Billy had expected a big number, that didn't seem like too much.

"Now, every time I look at that patch, every time I put up this tent, even before I see the patch, I think about my mistake and I make sure to pitch the tent far enough away from the fire to be safe."

He got up and walked around to the other side of the tent. He shined the light on the new hole, and then back over towards where his hole and patch were. Moving the light back and forth he said, "My hole, your hole, my mistake, your mistake, my lesson, your lesson."

Billy almost smiled.

"Tomorrow I'll show you how to patch it. Since my mistake I bring a patch kit with me. When I burnt that hole I didn't have a kit, so I got wet when it rained. You're lucky, since I've got a patch, unless it rains tonight, you're going to stay dry. But from now on I sleep under my hole and you sleep under yours. Okay?"

Billy smiled. "Okay."

Williams laughed and said, "Can you imagine what this tent is going to look like once Mike and Andrew burn their holes?"

With that, Billy burst out laughing.

Chapter 34

A few weeks later school started and the family settled into a routine. The boys seemed to be adjusting to their new lives. Increasingly, Betsy became apart of those lives. She loved reading with them, playing with them and helping them with their homework. She also loved cooking for them and kept the house beautifully. With more and more frequency, she stayed for dinner and lingered after, helping the boys with their homework and talking with Jim.

She grew to hate the weekends, her days off and made excuses to come by.

On weekends Jim almost never went out. If he did it was with the boys to a movie or to a pizza place or something of that nature. One Saturday Jim asked the boys if they wanted to go see the latest Star Wars movie. They said they did and that Betsy had been talking about it. Mike asked if she could come with them.

Jim thought about it. He didn't want to impose on her, it was her time off after all, but he knew her life really revolved around them. He sensed that she hated the weekends, hated being away from the boys and that she was lonely without them. So he told Mike to call her and see if she wanted to come along.

"Hi, Betsy. It's Mike."

"Hi, Mike."

"We're going to go see the new Star Wars. Do you want to come?"

"Sure, do you need a ride?"

"No. Dad's going to drive."

"You mean you want me to come with all of you?"

"Yeah, you've been talking about this movie forever. You should come."

"Why don't you put your dad on?"

"Dad, Betsy wants to talk to you."

Charlie

Jim reluctantly took the phone, embarrassed. "Hi Betsy, I don't mean to impose, and you don't have to come, but the boys and I are going to see the new Star Wars and then grab some dinner. They said you have been talking about it forever, so we figured you might want to come with us. But really, you don't have to, you spend so much time with us as it is. Please don't feel you have to come."

"I'd love to come. Really, I have nothing to do tonight. Thank you for thinking of me."

Jim smiled to himself, loving her honesty.

"Okay. We'll pick you up in about fifteen minutes."

"Fifteen minutes?"

"Yeah the movie starts at 6:30 over in Stratford, at the multiplex. We figured we'd go to the Spaghetti Factory afterwards."

"Okay, I'll see you then." She hung up abruptly.

About twelve minutes later they were in her driveway and Billy rang her doorbell. It took her about two minutes to answer and when she did she looked flustered, but happy.

At the theater she held Andrew, who was now a little over a year old. Billy and Mike sat on either side of her. Jim sat on the other side of Mike. During the movie, when Andrew got antsy she and Jim took turns going out into the lobby with him and would fill each other in during the switchovers.

Afterwards they went to dinner, looking and feeling like a family.

Chapter 35

From the start Betsy had fallen in love with the boys and with Jim. She believed in his innocence and saw his heart and his strength. Where others saw aloofness, she saw thoughtfulness and consideration.

Susan's murder had shown Jim how fleeting and ridiculous peoples' perceptions were and as a result he had simply stopped caring about them, to the extent he ever had. He just lived every day trying to do the best job he could. At the plant he worked hard and thoughtfully, getting things done in the most efficient way he could, not caring about credit or approval but about results. With the way Griesch had structured Square Box, with everyone benefitting from efficiency and working in such close proximity, credit naturally found its rightful owner. Accordingly with time, he assumed more and more responsibility at the plant and became a great team player and leader at once. He knew his own strengths and his own limitations and was quick to share praise and, when rarely due, shoulder blame. As a consequence he earned the respect of almost everyone at Square Box.

The men who worked with and for him came to realize that in spite of the rumors about him, he was someone they could trust. They knew he was slow to smile, so making him smile or better still laugh became an ongoing challenge.

At home he was equally disciplined. From the time of the camping trip he had seen the benefit of controlling his temper and he worked hard to do it. The loss of their mother had and would take an incalculable toll on his boys and he knew that while he wanted to teach them discipline and self-reliance, he had to try to always err on the side of compassion. They deserved and desperately needed that. And compassion was what he found and admired in Betsy.

She was a competent, secure, kind woman who simply wanted to give and to love. Jim saw that in her from the day she met the boys. She had been

Charlie

right that first day in Greisch's office. She could help him, help them and from the start she did. She taught and loved and cared, in part filling the void left by Susan's death. And she was also smart and honest. She didn't coddle the boys, but they quickly grew to know that her kindness and eventually her love was a given. She understood their father's disciplined nature and worked to instill it in the boys, giving them daily jobs like making their beds and helping with the dishes from an early age. But most of all she was fun. She loved to laugh and smile and play.

So almost from the start Jim and Betsy admired each other and with Betsy the admiration quickly turned to love. But she kept her feelings to herself. She had always been the sort of girl men liked to have as a friend, but was never the girl they asked out. With the boys she found a natural outlet for the maternal love she desperately wanted to give and she did not want to do anything to jeopardize that. And so she kept her growing feelings for Jim to herself.

The night Mike called and asked her if she wanted to join them to see Star Wars was a dream come true for her. She was bored and lonely on the weekends and spent them wondering what they were doing. Though he never showed it, she knew Jim must be lonely, too. She saw the way people treated him and was sure it must be taking its toll on him. Like his boys, he needed someone to simply love him.

After the first night at Star Wars, they asked her to join them again the next Saturday night and after that, it just became part of their routine. And as time progressed she ate more and more dinners with them during the week. It was just a natural sort of evolution. Any sense of her being an outsider or intruding on their privacy passed and her presence simply made sense. She often stayed for dinner and for the clean up afterwards, and sometimes stayed until after the boys had gone to bed.

One night after Jim finished reading to the boys she was putting on her coat to leave.

"Betsy, do you have a minute?"

"Sure, of course."

"Why don't you take your coat off? If you have a few minutes, there is something I'd like to discuss with you."

She felt her heart racing. In the nine months she had been with him, he had rarely spoken to her alone. He was so serious that she was afraid that she might have done something wrong.

He led her into the family room and they sat, she on the couch and he in an armchair.

"I have been worried about something for a while now and I figured I should just ask you about it."

"Yes of course, is something wrong?"

He could see the alarm in her eyes and immediately tried to reassure her. "Oh no, no not at all. It's just that I have been afraid that we are taking advantage of you, Betsy, the boys and me too. You spend so much time here."

She still felt her heart racing. She had been so happy for these past months and did want anything to change. She listened to his words, to his reassurance, but her thoughts rushed ahead. She thought he was going to fire her.

"Am I here too much? Am I intruding? I don't mean to."

He saw her concern grow and his efforts to console her fail. "Too much? Intruding? I feel as though we are intruding on you. You're doing a great job, I don't know what any of us would do without you."

His words slowly sank in. She tried to calm herself, to slow her thoughts down. She desperately wanted to question him, to find out what the looming "but" was, but instead composed herself and simply listened.

"Thank you."

He smiled and tried to get his point out. She could see that he was struggling and again had to try to force herself not to fear the worse. For as long as she remembered men she cared about had this effect on her. Her normally secure ego could be turned to mush with a simple turn of a head.

"There are a couple of issues I think we need to discuss . . . three actually."

She nodded, but didn't speak.

"The first is I want to be sure we are not taking too much advantage of you. You are doing a great job here. You must know that. I don't how I would have made it without you. As hard as this has all been, after all they have been through, the boys seem to be adjusting, even Billy."

She wanted to comment, to talk to him about each of the boys, about Billy especially, she had for months, but she did not want to overstep her bounds. So again she just listened.

"I want to be sure that you are happy with us. I think you are, Betsy, but you're such a kind person, I am not sure you would tell me if you weren't. So are you? Are you happy? Are we taking too much of your time?"

As he spoke he saw the tension in her face melt away.

Charlie

"Of course I am." She paused for a moment then went on. "I am so happy. You must know I just love the boys, I couldn't be happier."

He looked at her, listening, watching. She was incredible. She was simply incredible. He did know she loved the boys. It was obvious. She loved them like a mother. He considered his feelings for her. He knew he admired her tremendously. She was so kind and intelligent and thoughtful. She was able to both give his boys the love they so desperately needed and at the same time maintain discipline and teach them to be responsible and hard working. He knew she tried to parent them the way she thought he wanted her to. As he considered it he realized that she was parenting them as much as he was. She was mothering them. And he realized that to an extent, she did not have to restrain herself too much to parent the way he would want her to because she valued the same things he did, honesty and hard work. But she also valued kindness and fun. While he liked those things, and tried to be kind, especially to his children, he knew that he was too introverted and more recently too suspicious of people to be able to come off as kind, let alone fun-loving. But she could. She was the sort of the perfect balance for him.

He considered whether he loved her. He knew she loved him. She was good about hiding it, but he knew she did. He admired her tremendously and cared about her. In fact as he thought about it aside from his boys and his in-laws, he probably cared more about her than anyone he knew. Until this point he had never really thought too much about her. She was an important part of his family, a vital part. They needed her. But did he love her?

She had beautiful eyes and when she smiled her whole face lit up. It made him smile just thinking about it. She was lovely. She was big and getting bigger, but really he didn't care. He didn't think about her sexually, but he realized he could if he let himself. Did he love her like a sister? Or was there more?

She cleared her throat and he realized his mind had been wandering.

"What about the weekends? Are they too much? We include you because . . . because it's more fun when you are here and because you seem to want to come, but do you really? Is it just too much?"

Her heart lit up. Had he just said it more fun when she was with them, much more fun? She tried to compose herself, but she didn't, instead she just blurted out her thoughts.

"Of course I want to come. I love being with you and the boys. I hate going home. I hate the weekends."

For a second she was afraid she had said too much, revealed too much of herself, of her feelings. Then he just smiled a rare smile and said, "Okay, good."

They sat there for a minute, letting the new status quo settle in. Finally she asked, "You said there were three things you wanted to discuss?"

He smiled again. "Yes. It's, well it's the boys. You spend as much time or more time with them than I do, Betsy, and I know how smart you are, how much you care for them. I want to know you thoughts. Am I coddling Billy too much, should I be tougher on Mike, and am I spending enough time with Andrew? I know you try to do things the way you think I want them done, and I appreciate that, I do, but I need your opinion. These boys have been through so much, Billy especially. I need your help to be sure I'm not missing things."

She listened and just loved him. He was so good with them, so thoughtful and disciplined. This seemingly hard, tough, aloof man considered his every action. And he did so not from a selfish perspective but from the perspective of his children. She knew he was intentionally going easy on Billy and lately she could see Billy taking advantage of it. She tried to subtly rein the boy in, but she did not want to undo what Jim was doing. Now she could discuss it with him, ask him.

"So what are you asking me?"

"Can I discuss these things with you? Do you want to get involved at that level?"

As he spoke he realized he was asking her if she wanted to help him parent them and so did she.

"Yes, of course you can."

For the next hour they talked about the boys, about each of them, areas where they seemed solid and soft spots. He was amazed by how much her thoughts melded with his and by how easy it was to talk to her. They had both been bottling up their feelings and for each of them it was cathartic to be able to discuss them, at least with regard to the boys.

Finally as that discussion was winding down, she asked, "You said there were three things you wanted to discuss, I think we're on two?"

He laughed. "We've already covered a lot of ground."

"Please don't stop now, you'll have me wondering all night."

He laughed again. "Well, I want to teach the boys to hunt, one at a time. Billy is about the age to start. I wanted to take him a way for a weekend soon, but I hate to ask the Andersons to come out and not be with them and not let Billy be with them."

"I'd love to watch the boys. Just tell me when."

They talked for a while longer and then realized it was 11 o'clock. As she stood to leave he helped her into her coat and walked her to the door. As she was leaving she turned and faced him, then leaned up and kissed him on his cheek.

"Thank you, Jim."

He just smiled and responded. "Thank you." Then he leaned down and kissed her cheek, too.

Chapter 36

A year later they were married.

For Jim the most difficult part of deciding whether to ask her to marry him had been gauging the feelings of Susan's parents. He knew the boys had grown to love her and thought that they would be ok with him marrying her. In fact he was sure they would be thrilled. But he was not as sure about his in-laws. They were still a big part of the boys' lives and Jim did not want to alienate them. So he asked them.

From the start the Andersons had liked Betsy and Emily had known early on that she was in love with her son-in-law. She and Frank continued to struggle with the loss of their daughter and with the fact that her killer had not been found, but they had been able to live believing in Jim's innocence. It was he who kept them in his family's life. He clearly did want them involved in their grandchildren's upbringing and they wanted it, too.

Even before he asked her to marry him, he had driven out to their suburban Philadelphia home, surprising them. He knew they would initially think his unexpected visit would mean that there was some new information with regard to the murder, but he felt any momentary disappointment they might feel from no news on that front was better than either asking for their blessing over the phone or pre-announcing his intention to visit without telling them the reason.

So he surprised them with his visit, but not with his question. In their hearts they both knew that Betsy was a sweet, kind, intelligent woman and that their grandchildren would be better off with her in their lives. So they suppressed their natural feelings of loss and blessed the marriage.

After he had spoken with the Andersons, he asked Betsy. Since that first night when he asked her to stay for a while they often sat together, discussing their days or the boys or whatever. When they went to the movies instead of sitting around the kids they sat together with the kids around them.

Charlie

Goodnight kisses on the cheeks evolved into soft kisses on the lips and they had slowly become a couple, comfortable with each other if not passionate.

Betsy knew she loved Jim differently and maybe more than Jim loved her. She knew too that a lot of people, people who assumed he was a killer, viewed her as flawed for being with him, especially as they started to be seen as a couple. Even her parents tried to warn her off of him. All of this did trouble her. When she allowed herself her most insecure thoughts she sometimes felt the only reason that a plain, heavy woman like her could attract a man like Jim was that he was tainted. And when she allowed those thoughts she feared for her relationship, feared that he was making do, compromising with her. She thought he loved her, but worried it was more admiration than passion. Even with those thoughts she was happier with him and the boys than she had ever been.

And so when one night he asked her if she would marry him she said yes, simply, honestly and immediately.

The adjustment seemed easy for the boys, too. Betsy had them call her Betsy, not Mom. She did not want them to feel she was trying to replace their mother in any way. She just wanted to make them happy. And generally she did. Andrew really only knew her. He was almost three now and did not have any memory of Susan. Mike adjusted well to her. Jim and Betsy were sure he missed his mother and Jim spoke openly about her with the boys, not wanting them to ever forget her. Betsy was good about it, too. She hadn't know Susan and never pretended she had, but she never left anyone feeling they shouldn't mention Susan or the things she did around her. Her parents had met the boys several times, but they felt no bond and with Jim's parents both gone, the Andersons were the boys only connection to their past. Betsy had grown to like them both and tried to make them feel as welcome as always. After their marriage, it was often she who contacted Emily to invite them for visits.

Billy was a different story. He had never admitted seeing his mother to anyone. While he generally appeared to get along well with his father, there were still times when he seemed to draw back from him. Jim had long since stopped coddling him, but even after all this time, because of what the boy had been through, he felt he had to let Billy get away with things he otherwise wouldn't. Billy was the unknown in the family. His sometimes sullen nature could drain the normal joy or at least happy feeling that Betsy had brought to their home.

Even in that way, he was like his father. Jim could get lost in himself, in his thoughts. Being treated as a murderer by many wore on him and at times he seemed happiest on his own, working things over and through. But marrying Betsy forced him to be more disciplined still. He loved the happiness she brought into the house and he did not want to discourage it with his dark moods. To temper those moods and to find time to himself, he would get up at about 5:00 each morning and take the dogs for a long walk along the quiet rural roads just beyond their subdivision. He loved watching them walk along together, sniffing and finding scents, just happy and carefree. Alone with them he could forget all that he had been through and the responsibilities he shouldered and just walk, guilt and burden free.

While he tried to use his morning walks to calm himself, at times during them his thoughts wondered back to that night three years ago. He had replayed it and the weeks and months leading up to it in his mind hundreds if not thousands of times. Each time, no matter how he replayed it, no matter how he tried to change the nuances of past events, she ended up dead.

Some mornings when he got up out of bed, Betsy would get up with him and even walk with him. He always tried to make her feel welcome and when he thought about it, often enjoyed her company during the walks, but she seemed to sense that they were his time. She knew, too, or at least thought, that that did not reflect badly on their relationship. Like many people, he just needed some time to himself, alone in his thoughts and she generally respected that. And truthfully while she always felt good after she got up and walked with him and the dogs, she preferred to sleep a little later, and especially in the cold winter months, to stay in the warmth of her bed.

Nonetheless, one sunny morning she decided to get up with him, partly because she was feeling fat and wanted to try to get her metabolism going first thing and partly because she just loved his company.

"Would you mind if I came with you this morning?"

He smiled at her, loving how considerate she was of his feelings and of those of the boys. "Come on, let's go. I love it when you come with me."

She smiled and started to get out of bed, her mind and heart grateful for his kindness, but her body fighting to keep her in the warm comfort of the covers. He saw her mind's battle and laughed. "Come on, lazy bones, get up."

He walked to her side of the bed and pulled her up kissing her now smiling face. She hugged him and tried to pull him back into the bed. He fell on top of her, laughing and rolling off her, still holding her, kissing her pretty face. "I thought you wanted to go for a walk."

"There are other forms of exercise you know."

He laughed again and drew her towards him.

Twenty minutes later they left the house, the unleashed dogs leading them on their familiar route.

Walking beside her, he touched her back and said, "This morning is the perfect way to start a day."

She slipped her hand into his and squeezed, as happy as she had ever been. She just walked along, feeling like a welcome guest with him and his dogs. She loved watching and being a part of their routine, but did not want to intrude on it or detract from it, so she just walked and observed, glad to be there.

He wasn't sure that she understood or felt the peace he felt in the quiet solitude of the early morning, but she did understand that he found comfort in it. She was so good that way, understanding or at least partially understanding and not needing more, not making it about her.

"You should come with me more often. It's nice having you here."

"I always love it when I do come, and I feel good about it for the rest of the day, but you know me, I like my warm bed. And you never make me feel this way, but I feel as though it's your time."

"But I love when you come."

She cut him off. "I know you do, and you always make that clear, but it is your time. I have my time, too, you know."

"You do? When?"

"After you go to work and the boys are off to school and Andy is settled playing."

"What do you do?"

"To make it really work, I have to get all the little stuff done. Clean up from breakfast, check the boys' rooms, get a load of laundry in. If I feel like I'm really on top of everything, I get a cup of coffee and a blanket and lay down on the couch and read, sometimes for an hour if I can. I feel like I'm stealing time."

"So I'm off working and the boys are at school and there you are, laying around?"

She laughed and nodded. "Like Cleopatra herself."

He laughed, too.

They walked quietly along, holding hands and happy.

Chapter 37

Billy heard the dogs and looked out his bedroom window. He was a little surprised to see Betsy walking with his father on his morning walk. He liked Betsy and had been pleased when they were married. She seemed to calm his father and he was glad of that.

Once he saw them turn off the driveway and head down the street he tiptoed out of his room and down into the basement. He checked the steps and then walked into a small storage closet in the back corner. Inside the closet he removed a piece of backing to one of the built-in shelves there, the lowest shelf, just off the floor. He reached his hand in behind the shelf and around to the left, feeling in a gap between the walls until he found what he was looking for, a shoe box, which he had resting on top of a small block of two-by-fours he had nailed together and placed there to keep the box off the ground.

He opened the box and took out a bunch of letters. They were all held together by two rubber bands. He unbound them and took out the top one, the one he read most often. He checked the door and then looked up the steps to make sure he was still alone, then settled down on the floor of the closet, near his hiding place. He carefully pulled the letter from its envelope and started to read.

Dear Susan,

Last night was better than ever. I love being with you, touching you, kissing you, being in you.

When we are together nothing else matters . . .

Billy skimmed through the next few paragraphs. They were, he had eventually concluded, nothing but romantic dribble. The writer went on and on about how much he loved her and how they were meant to be together. He skipped down to the part he read most often.

> *When you said last week that you did not want to see me anymore, that you couldn't do it to your husband and kids anymore, you must have know the impact it would have on me. You don't have to be afraid of him. His threats are empty. I can protect you. Even if he knows, it doesn't matter. We don't have to take the next steps I asked you about. Let's just continue to meet when he goes away or when you can get away for an hour or two. We don't have to change anything. Stay with him if you feel you have to, but don't stop being with me. You need me as much as I need you.*
>
> *I love you.*

The note, like all of the others, was unsigned.

Months before she was killed Billy had seen his mother taping a packet of notes to the back of one of the drawers of her dresser. A month or two after her death, after they had moved back into their house on Milmar, he had taken the drawer out and found them.

When he first read them he had been confused.

He was sure that there had been times when he had heard the voice of a strange man in the house. They were on nights when his dad was away, so he was afraid. Sometimes there had been laughing and other times arguing. A few times he had tried to go out to see what was happening, but his door had been blocked. Once, on a night when he heard yelling, he had even called out to his mom. He remembered the yelling becoming hushed and then hearing the back door slam. A few moments later his mom had come in and reassured him that everything was ok.

But on the night, the last night, he could not remember hearing the other man. He remembered his parents arguing, really having it out right after dinner. They were arguing about the man. He heard his father refer to him, heard him say she had to stop seeing him. A while after that, things had seemed calm. His dad had come in and read to him and Mike and an hour or two later he remembered hearing him drive away. Later he woke up and heard her arguing again, his father must have come back. He tried to get out of his room, out to them, but had again found his door blocked. He had called to them and for a minute the arguing stopped. He heard them walk by his room, from the bedroom down to the family room. Then he heard her scream.

Chief Mason and various other policemen and lawyers and doctors had often asked him about the night, but he had decided not to tell them anything, not about the other man or even about the notes when he later found them.

Originally he hadn't wanted to speak because he was afraid. When he saw his mother that next morning he knew that his father had done it. He was afraid that if he said a word his father would kill him, too. As much as he had loved his dad, he had always feared his temper. Billy had never seen him strike his mom or him or his brothers, but he sure could scare them with his cold stares.

So he decided to keep quiet. For quite a while he lived in fear, thinking that his father and everyone else knew he wouldn't have left the house without walking into the family room. His dad knew that he had seen her and must have heard them arguing. Billy was sure that at some point he would confront him. For the first few weeks his grandparents had been there to protect him. When they left, he was terrified. But nothing happened. His father actually seemed to be making a serious effort not to show his temper at all.

With time he grew to believe that his father was too smart to risk killing him. And he took comfort in that. At times he even forgot and treated his father the way he used to, adoring him, worshipping him. He saw too that his father was now cautious around him. He was able to get away with things he never would have before. He knew that people felt having seen his mother's body had scarred him and that as a result they treated him carefully. And it wasn't only his father. He was surprised to see how deferentially teachers and adults in general treated him. He subtly took advantage of it. Most of the time he was well behaved and quiet, but he knew he could get away with things others couldn't and he used it to his advantage.

The first time he had noticed was when he had gone camping with his father and burnt a hole in the tent. In the old days, while his father might not have been mad about the tent itself, he would have been furious about the way it had happened. He would have made Billy describe how he was running around with the flaming stick and forced him to deduct that something bad was inevitably going to happen as a consequence. That night however, he had visibly calmed himself and then methodically shown Billy his own earlier mistake. That moment and that whole trip had been the first time that Billy had fallen back into treating his father the old way, for more than a moment at least. And he had seen how his father reacted. It had been as if a huge load had been lifted from his back. Billy had felt a sense of power in that moment. He knew that he could manipulate the situation to his advantage. He would

Charlie

have to be subtle, his father was too smart to be easily duped, but he was so desperate for Billy's love that Billy knew he could, in fact, be duped. He had considered whether his desperation came from true paternal love or from a need to believe that the murder of his mother could be put behind him, behind them. In the end, however, he didn't care. He knew his dad had killed her. He would carefully, slowly lull his father into a false confidence. At times he would intentionally slip back into a sullen mood and in so doing keep his father in line, remind him of his guilt. Other times he would behave normally towards him, as if nothing had happened. But he would always remember and never, ever forgive. In fact, he thought that in time, he would even avenge her death.

Chapter 38

Each summer the boys would spend a week or two with their grandparents. As they had in previous years, in the fourth summer after Susan's death the Andersons' took them to their cottage on the Jersey Shore. The cottage was within walking distance of town and sometimes after dinner Frank and Emily would let Billy and Mike go into town on their own. The boys liked to wander around and look at the boats in the marina and wander through the junky tourist shops in the area.

One night they were running along the docks, chasing each other, dodging tourists and touching every dock post and bench, the way kids often do. In one nicer section of the docks, the tee shirt shops ended and art galleries started. Billy led Mike into that area and as they ran past one gallery Billy pushed off of a five foot tall carved turtle holding an umbrella. When he pushed the statue fell and the umbrella broke off.

For a moment the boys stopped, staring. Several onlookers who had seen the innocent mistake started to approach. Billy looked at the broken statue and the oncoming adults and made a decision. He grabbed Mike's hand and ran, pulling him away. A few of the adults yelled after them, but none followed. Holding tight to his brother's wrist, Billy ran and ran, until they were in the outskirts of the small tourist town among the nearby homes.

"Billy, you broke that statue. We've got to go back and tell them."

"Are you crazy? We can't go back there."

"But we have to. It was an accident, you didn't mean to break it."

"Me? I didn't break it, we broke it."

"I didn't even touch it, Billy. You did."

"We were both running. We both broke it, Mike. If we get caught, we are both in huge trouble. Do you know how much the stuff at those stores costs? If they find about it was us, we'll have to pay for it. Dad will have to pay for it."

"But I didn't do anything. You broke it."

Billy stood over Mike, intentionally intimidating his younger, smaller brother.

"We're not going to say a word about this, Mike. You can't tell Grandma or Grandpa and you definitely can never tell Dad or Betsy. We're leaving in three days. All we have to do is stay out of town for the next three days and we'll be fine."

"But you know on our last night Grandma and Grandpa always bring us down to the docks for ice cream."

"Well this year we just won't go. I'll take care of it. You just keep your mouth shut."

Mike looked up at him, scared, both of the trouble they might get in and of his brother.

"I mean it, Mike. I don't want you to say one word. Do you hear me? All we have to do is be quiet and everything will be fine."

Mike just nodded.

The boys made their way back to the house, staying away from the docks and walking along the outskirts of the town. Their grandparents were surprised to see the boys home early, but were pleased when Billy and Mike joined them for a game of Hearts before bed.

For the next two days, Billy stayed with Mike, not leaving him alone with his grandparents. On the last night after dinner, when the Andersons enthusiastically suggested they all walk into town for their traditional last night ice cream cones, the two older boys pretended to have stomachaches. Frank walked Andy into town while Emily stayed home with the boys.

When Frank got home, he had hand-packed ice cream for the two older boys and for Emily. By then the boys stomachaches had passed, and as they sat eating their treat, Billy smiled a chilling smile at his younger brother. He had manipulated the situation perfectly.

The next day they left.

Chapter 39

As the boys aged, Billy's influence over his brothers grew. In high school he did well academically and in sports and his younger brothers naturally looked up to him.

He and his brothers were all treated differently than the other students. The kid gloves with which they had been handled in the years immediately following their mother's murder had long since passed, but the stigma of being associated with murder had not. While Jim's no-nonsense personality and tremendous work ethic earned him respect at Square Box, the respect did not translate into general social acceptance. The better families of Harrison, the "nice" families, did not want to associate with a potential murderer. And in spite of Betsy's endless work volunteering at the boys' schools and no matter how well the boys did in class or on the sports fields, she and the boys were also treated differently.

There were events at which Jim and Betsy Williams were acceptable company. If the parents of the high school football team gathered for a dinner, they would be invited and even treated well. In fact, for school related events in general, they were welcome. However, with any subsection of those larger groups, they were generally not included. If four or five couples went out after an event, or especially if they met at someone's house, the Williams were excluded. With time Jim and Betsy learned to avoid making it awkward for people. As a game neared its end, if couples started to discuss plans, the Williams would turn away or talk to each other. At first Betsy had resented it and even tried to insert herself and Jim into the events. But with time her resentment at being excluded turned to apathy and disinterest. Like her husband, she did not want to go where she wasn't truly wanted.

She had friends of her own and there were several couples who didn't care what other people thought, but generally, Jim and Betsy led a private life

Charlie

together. They would go to games and school events and even to some of the large social gatherings, but they were always among the first to leave.

Jeff and Amy Griesch were acutely aware of Jim and Betsy's situation and tried to diffuse it. Given Jeff's role as one of the area's largest employers, the Grieschs held considerable social sway. In the early days they included Jim and Betsy in dinner parties and other events, but truthfully, neither Williams fit into the same social group as the Griesch's. Consequently, after a few painful but well-intentioned nights, Betsy would politely refuse Amy's invitations, always finding a schedule conflict.

So the couple settled into a quiet, but relatively happy life. Jim never had been very social and while Betsy was much more outgoing, she was deeply in love with her husband and loved time with him. She kept herself busy on school and church committees during the day and was very content being with her family at night and on the weekends.

For the boys, the situation was more variable. All three boys developed into good athletes and found the easy social acceptance associated with that. They also developed the politeness shared by both their surrogate mother and their father. For Mike and Andy, that politeness came pretty naturally. For Billy, now Bill, it was more forced.

Like most towns, Harrison had different social strata. Generally the layers were divided by a combination of wealth and education. For kids, the delineations were blurred, especially at young ages. However, with time and intensity of association, the lines became clearer. For example, even when the boys were young, if one of their friends had a group of friends over to play, the Williams boys were generally welcome. If only one friend was invited to play, the Williams boys were to be avoided. There had been many times when one of the boys had made plans to play with some new friend, only to have the friend's mother find a convenient excuse to cancel the plans once she learned a Williams boy was involved. As with the parents, there were families who would overlook the rumors about the father for the sake of the little boys, but in so doing they risked being ostracized themselves. And on top of that, even parents who would welcome the Williams boys into their own homes felt nervous about allowing their young children to play at the house of a man who may or may not have committed murder.

As a result, in spite of Betsy's best efforts, genuine kindness and great baking, the Williams house was never a play date destination or in later years, a place where kids would go. While all of this was subtle, none of it escaped the boys. It was all part of the price of having their mother murdered.

Their unacceptable status was especially apparent when it came to dating. Few fathers liked the idea of their daughter dating a Williams boy. As a result the girls they did date generally had parents who either kept a very close eye on things or didn't care at all.

So for the boys, life was complicated and at times unfair. This wore on Bill in particular. He was the guinea pig; the testing grounds for peoples' acceptance or more accurately, their lack of acceptance. He was smart enough to recognize false kindness and became increasingly cynical and bitter. He hid it, but it was there, always. Many of his problems stemmed from his mother's murder and his hidden hatred focused on her murderer, his father.

Chapter 40

In some ways Jim Williams had moved on, but really that single night so many years ago still defined him and had more of an impact then all the other days of his life combined.

He was happy with Betsy. He had grown to truly love her. She was patient and understanding and remarkably smart. The boys loved her, too, and had come to count on her. She was a good loving mother to them. She also understood what they were going through because she felt the same pressures and exclusions that they did. From her own parents' reactions when she had married Jim, she knew that some people would be difficult, but she had underestimated how pervasive the intolerance would be. Prior to marrying Jim, while she had never been wealthy, she had been part of the educated, professional Christian community in her town, Greenville, and as such was an acceptable guest pretty much anywhere. However, for her that all changed, too. Many of her prior friends quietly avoided being with her and Jim and while some were still willing to do things with her individually, she did not want to remain friends on those terms. And likewise, she saw how many families rejected the boys. It broke her heart when the boys would make after school plans with some new buddy at school only to have the child's mother quash the idea. She watched as even at a young age, the kids learned to work around their history.

Even with all of that she was happy. She loved her life with them and in turn, tried to make each of their lives as full of love as they would allow. And this, more than all of her many other great qualities, was what Jim loved most about her. She just gave and gave. And unlike with some people, for her the act of giving was reward enough. She looked for no payback, for no reward. It was sort of like his work ethic. He didn't care about receiving credit. He just liked to do a job well. She was the same way.

Together they tried to both shield the boys and let them experience life. Their coddling of Billy had long since ended. They had seen him take advantage of it and tried, perhaps too late, to change things.

When Billy was in eleventh grade, Betsy received a call from the high school Principal's office. Billy and two other boys had been involved in a bullying incident and the principal wanted to meet with the three and their parents that day at five.

Betsy called Jim, and he left work early to get to the school on time. He met Billy and Betsy in front of the school and was surprised by the cold look he got from his son. As he had long since conditioned himself to do, he withheld any comment until he was fully aware of the facts, but in truth, he hadn't been shocked when Betsy told him that Billy had been accused of bullying.

The Williams and the two other families gathered outside the principal's office and were led into a nearby conference room. In the room the families sort of split up, each parent both guarding and quietly interrogating their own son. Within a minute, however, the interrogations were cut short as the principal and vice principal entered along with another set of parents, who turned out to be the "victim's" mother and father.

The principal, George Walmont, started the meeting.

"Thank you all for coming. I'm sorry to have to ask you to be here, but your sons have been accused of bullying a freshman girl, and that is something we just can't tolerate here."

The father of one of the boys, Rick Hume interrupted the principal. Hume was from one of Harrison's "good" families and was not used to being on the wrong side of a situation like this.

"Mr. Walmont, my son didn't bully anyone. I find this whole thing to be . . "

Walmont interrupted right back. "Mr. Hume, please. Let me just lay out what happened."

Hume settled in and gave the appearance that he was willing to listen, for a moment at least.

"This afternoon between the 1:10 and 1:15 class bells the Nelson's daughter Tina was walking down the main second floor corridor." The stern, accusing looks on the victim's parents' faces turned sterner still at the mention of their daughter' name.

"She was walking with two other freshman girls. Apparently the three young girls were walking in the opposite direction of your three sons. Rather than share the common space, the boys formed a wall and forced the girls to sort of squeeze through. As Tina was coming through apparently one of the boys, I think Bill Williams, elbowed her books up against her face. A textbook hit her face so hard that her nose started to bleed."

The two other boys' parents' expressions turned from innocent defiance directed at the principal to indignation directed at the Williams.

"The boys apparently all burst out laughing and kicked her now dropped books all over the hallway."

He stopped and let that sink in. The indignation toned down a bit, but just a bit.

"We just can't let this sort of behavior go on. You must all understand that. Your sons are sophomores and juniors and this is a girl, and a small freshman girl at that. This sort of bullying is simply unacceptable."

Hume spoke up again. "Listen, I couldn't agree more. There is no way that behavior like this is acceptable, but there is a difference between hitting someone and kicking her books, if her books were even purposely kicked."

The other non-hitting, non-victim parents, the Sinclairs, nodded and muttered their agreement. All eyes turned to the Williams.

Principal Walmont spoke again. "Bill, why don't you tell us what happened?"

Bill sat there for a moment, gathering his thoughts. Unlike the other two boys he didn't seem at all nervous.

"The way you said things happened is sort of true, Mr. Walmont."

All of the adults in the room, except for Jim and Betsy, were taken back by the boy's words.

"Ted and Chris and I were walking down the hall between classes and we were goofing around. I guess I was flailing my arms and I did hit Tina's books, but I sure didn't mean to. And the guys did laugh, but they were laughing at me, not at Tina, at me for being so clumsy. And as soon as we saw the blood on Tina's face, the laughing stopped."

With several sentences Bill had both admitted but diminished his own guilt and exonerated his friends. The other boys' parents' prior indignation quickly turned to nodding agreement and now a hint of concern for poor Tina. It was all just an innocent accident and if there was any blame it did not fall on their sons. Bill did hit her books, but it was all just an accident.

The principal interrupted. "That's not the way Tina's friends saw it, Bill. They said you hit her books on purpose."

"It's just not true, sir. I was talking about something, flailing my hands. We must have passed a dozen other people in that tight space. I didn't even really notice Tina or her friends until I accidently hit her books. I don't even know her. Why would I want to hurt her?"

Everyone in the room sat quietly for a moment.

Bill turned to Tina's parents, looking directly into their eyes as he spoke. "Mr. and Mrs. Nelson, I'm so sorry. I know I did this. I hurt her, but it was an accident. Please tell her how sorry I am."

He kept it short and simple.

The Nelsons turned to the other boys. "But you laughed. Why?"

Ted Hume spoke for them. "It is like Bill said Mr. Nelson, we were laughing at Bill for being such a klutz, not at Tina, sir."

"Why didn't you help her afterwards?"

Bill spoke again. "We should have, sir. I know that now. But Tina's two friends grouped around her and sort of blocked us out. Also, and I know this is wrong, but boys get so many bloody noses and cuts and bruises from just goofing around that I didn't think it was that big of a deal. And I did gather her books for her afterwards, sir. I gave them to one of her two friends."

The adults in the room all looked at each other, seeming generally satisfied. Eventually all eyes turned back to the Nelsons. They looked at each other and then at the principal. Mr. Nelson nodded.

Walmont judiciously accepted his nod and then somberly addressed the room.

"Clearly Bill here should not have been moving so aggressively through the corridors, but I think we can all agree that this was not a case of bullying. I don't think Ted or Chris did anything wrong. You two are excused. Thanks to you and your parents for coming in."

He turned to Bill. "Bill, I think you should go to detention this week, for three days. And I would appreciate it if you would be more careful in the corridors."

"Yes, sir."

With that they all got up to leave. The fathers of the other two boys walked up to Bill and shook his hand, thanking him for his honesty. Jim and Betsy stood back quietly.

Detention for that day had already come and gone, so Bill left with his father and Betsy. In the parking lot as Jim and Betsy split up to head to their own cars Jim said, "Bill, why don't you ride home with me?"

Charlie

Bill looked at him tentatively. "Actually, I was going to hang around here for a while and then catch a ride home with Ted."

"Get in the car."

Betsy just watched. Billy walked around to the passenger side of his father's van. Jim was quiet as he made his way out of the parking lot.

"You manipulated that pretty well."

"What do you mean?"

"You know exactly what I mean. You just appeased everyone in that room, but don't think you fooled me."

"You think I hit her on purpose?"

"I know you did."

They were quiet for a minute. Jim wasn't sure what to do. "Look, Bill, I've watched you massage the truth and manipulate things for a long time now and it's got to stop."

"What are you talking about?" Bill was almost laughing. "I didn't do a thing."

"Look, you can't go through life playing with people and working around the truth. It will catch up with you."

Bill was quiet for a while and then said.

"It hasn't caught up with you."

They were both quiet, silent.

Williams pulled over and turned to face his son. "What do you mean?"

"You know exactly what I mean."

"No, I don't."

"Look what you got away with. You manipulated things perfectly. Perfectly."

"What things? What are you talking about?"

"About Mom. I know you did it."

Williams just sat there, staring at his seventeen-year-old son. "Are you saying that you think I killed your mother?"

The boy stared straight into his eyes. "I know you did."

The father looked forward, out the front window. Then he turned back to face his son. "I know you did, Billy."

The two sat there, staring right into each other's eyes, so similar and so different. After a few minutes, Williams put the car back into gear and drove home.

Chapter 41

After that, Bill and his father hardly spoke. Betsy questioned Jim about what had happened but he couldn't bring himself to tell her.

The family dynamic changed, too. For a while Jim found excuses to work late and skip the family dinner. Mike and Andy knew something dramatic had happened between the two, but like Betsy, they didn't know exactly what.

Betsy saw the change spreading beyond Billy and Jim and worked to draw them back in, before things deteriorated further.

One morning about a week after the meeting at the school, Betsy got up with Jim to go for his morning walk. He saw through her motives and at first wasn't as welcoming as he normally had been. For the first ten minutes, they walked in silence. She just held his hand, waiting him out. As always he led them out of the subdivision onto the winding rural road at its north end.

He tried to ignore her silence, but eventually he spoke.

"You know as well as I do that he manipulated everyone in that room."

"Yes, I know he did."

"Well, I've had enough. He's going to have to learn to be accountable for his actions. We have to stop him."

Betsy didn't quite understand what he meant. "What happened, Jim? What happened in the car?"

Jim was torn. He couldn't tell her what he and Billy had said. She had never doubted his innocence. She was the one person who truly believed in him. He didn't think he could stand her doubt too. Nor could he tell her what he really thought.

"I told him I knew he worked that situation. We fought about it."

They walked for a while longer. She knew he had more to say and let him gather his thoughts.

Charlie

He gripped her hand tightly. "Do you remember the night, the first night I asked you to stay late with me, before we were married?"

"The three questions? Of course I do."

"Remember when we were talking about whether we were overly coddling Billy because of all that he must have seen?"

"Sure, and I guess we both know that we did over coddle him. I know he manipulated the principal and all those people last week, too, Jim."

"I confronted him on it."

"What did he say?"

Williams was quiet.

"We argued. All these years we have treated him too softly, let him get away with things we shouldn't have. He thinks he can do whatever he wants. He can't."

He paused for a while and then said, "I've lost him, Betsy."

"How?"

Again he went silent.

Chapter 42

After that Jim did come home for dinners and Betsy worked to mend the fence between the two men, but it wasn't easy. Mike and Andy tried, too, filling the voids in conversations and doing their best to keep things light and happy.

Bill acted as though nothing had happened. He would even try to engage his father, talking about school or practice or the Pirates. Jim would listen and for the sake of the rest of his family even respond at times, but they all knew things were different.

To try to keep things normal with Mike and Andy at least, Jim continued his long tradition of taking them away for hunting and fishing weekends. They traveled all over Pennsylvania, but their favorite spot remained the area up around Concord where Jim had been found after Susan's death.

He and the boys had been there so many times that over the years they had gotten to know some of the families who had cabins in the area. One family in particular, the Hendries, had spent a lot of time hunting with the Williams. But Mr. Hendrie's kids were older and for the last few years, from October through May, he and his wife Jill went to Florida. Mr. Hendrie, Geoff, had offered Jim the use of the cabin, and at times if the weather was particularly harsh, Jim had taken him up on it. Even if he didn't stay there, Jim would park at Geoff's and check on both the cabin and his Ford Bronco II. Geoff asked Jim to run it periodically just to give the engine some work.

A few weeks after Jim and Billy's confrontation, the four Williams men had scheduled a camping trip to the Concord area. But on the Thursday they were scheduled to leave, Griesch asked Jim to stay around for the weekend, to help reconfigure the production line at the plant to meet a huge non-standard order. Jim had to agree and told the boys at dinner that night.

Betsy could see the disappointment on the boys' faces. "That's such a shame."

After a minute, Bill asked, "Can't we still go?"

"No, you're too young to go away hunting on your own."

"I didn't mean hunting. I mean just go camping and fishing."

At this point, the boys were seventeen, fifteen and eight, respectively. While there was no question of Andy going, Jim and Betsy considered allowing the two older boys to go.

Betsy, who was still trying to mend things, spoke next. "Andy, I'm afraid you can't go. But Jim, what do you think about letting Billy and Mike go, just for one night? They could get up early on Saturday and head up." She turned to the boys. "You two could fish and camp for one night and come home Sunday afternoon."

The boys looked excitedly towards their father. Jim was a little surprised that Betsy was putting him in this position, but he knew she was trying to re-establish the normal happiness that she had long since brought to their family. Still, he had been shaken by Billy's actions and was not sure he wanted to trust him.

"I don't know."

Mike spoke up. "Come on, Dad, you know we can handle it."

"It's a long drive up there. I'm just not comfortable with you guys driving that far alone."

Everyone was quiet for a moment and then to break the building tension Betsy said, "How about if I take them?"

All four men burst out laughing. After he contained his laughter, Mike spoke next, asking, "You want to go camping?"

"No, I don't want to go camping. And I'm not going to go. While Dad works the four of us can drive up to Concord. Andy and I can stay at the Hendries' cabin and you two can camp out. During the day you can take Andy out with you, and he can spend the night in the cabin with me. You guys can either eat with me or cook your own dinner. But Andy stays with me."

Andy said, "Come on, I want to camp with them."

"There is not a chance I'm staying by myself in that cabin. Andy, you are staying with me, and so are at least two of the dogs."

They all laughed at that, too. At the very least, she had accomplished that.

After some discussion the boys all agreed and they all turned to Jim. "I think it's a great idea, but I want to come, too. Why don't we wait until next weekend and then we can all go and for two nights?" He turned to the two older boys, addressing Billy directly in the nicest tone he had since before the car ride. "You two can camp out alone both nights. I think that's a good idea actually. You're ready for it. Betsy and Andy and I will stay at the cabin."

Betsy jumped in next. "That's perfect. And if you're going then I don't need to go."

They all jumped on that. "No way, you're coming."

Happily defeated, she acquiesced.

So the next weekend the five of them headed up to Concord. Jim had called Geoff Hendrie to make sure he was okay with the idea. He was thrilled to have the place used and knew that Jim would leave it better than he found it. He too had been a beneficiary of Jim's quiet fixes.

They got there Friday afternoon and Billy and Mike headed out, taking two dogs with them. The other three stayed in the cabin, playing cards and eating and having fun.

On Saturday, they all hooked up and hiked and fished around the area. The boys took pride in showing Betsy the area and their considerable outdoor skills. They all had dinner at the boy's campsite, eating the trout they caught that day, and then Jim and Betsy and Andy headed back to the cabin.

About thirty minutes after they left, Billy began to unfold his long plotted plan. Sitting by the fire with Mike he started.

"Do you remember Mom much?"

"Yeah, pretty much. I remember how pretty she was."

"Yeah, she sure was, and so nice, too."

He let Mike tell him some of the stories he remembered about her, going slowly.

"Do you remember how Dad used to fight with her?"

"Not really. Did they fight a lot?"

"Oh yeah, you have to remember. Dad was always riding her, yelling at her about everything."

Mike knew how Billy could spin things when he wanted to, but he did seem to remember some screaming between his parents.

"Do you remember the morning when we found out she was dead? When we went over to the Bacons'?"

Mike thought for a moment. "Yes, I can still remember Mr. Bacon waking me up and carrying me to his house. And then we stayed there for a few days. Dad and I fixed the Bacon's doorbell."

"That was only after Dad got home. He spent the first few days after Mom was killed in jail."

Charlie

"I know, Billy. I've heard all those bullshit stories. But he didn't do it."

Bill paused for a long time then said, "I've never told anyone this Mike, but he did."

"What are you talking about?"

"You can never tell anyone what I'm going to tell you. Ever."

Mike looked at him skeptically. "You're so full of shit."

"I'm telling you he killed her."

"Dad? No way."

"He did."

"How would you know?"

"You can't tell anyone any of this."

"Any of what?"

"Promise me, you can't tell anyone, not even Betsy, do you promise?"

"Fine. I won't tell anyone. I don't believe you, anyway."

"Just listen first, then decide."

Mike kicked at the fire and leaned back to listen.

"Do you remember that when Mr. Bacon came to get you I was already gone?"

"Yeah, I guess so."

In all the years the boys had never talked about this before and as they progressed, Mike wasn't sure he wanted to now.

"Well, that's because I went to get Mr. Bacon."

"Okay."

"Before I left I saw Mom."

At first Mike didn't say anything. He knew this was probably true, he had heard talk over the years.

"What did you see?"

This part was hard for Billy. It was true, but he had to be careful. "I saw her body, Mike. She was dead, beaten and bloody. It was awful."

Mike felt bad for his brother, it must have been horrible, but he had always wanted to know.

"I heard she was killed with a hammer. Is that right?"

Billy smiled inwardly. He was turning into a source of information now. He was credible. He would stay with what he was sure was the truth for as long as he could.

"Yeah, Dad's hammer. I saw it, right beside her body. It was all covered in blood." Again he paused, as if he was picturing it all in his head. "I was staring at her body. It was so awful, I couldn't understand at first, but I couldn't look away. Then I sort of regained my focus and started to look around. I can remember as clear as day Mike. I looked away from her and the next thing I saw were the initials "JW". I saw the letters before I even realized what they were. Then I saw that they were Dad's initials on his hammer. It all went so slowly. I remember realizing right then that he killed her."

The younger brother just listened.

"It was awful, Mike. He hit her with it so many times."

Mike sat there, thinking, processing all that he was hearing. After about twenty seconds, he said, "If it was his hammer and he was arrested, why did he get out of jail? The police must have found all of that stuff. If Dad did it, he would still be in jail."

"They thought he did it, they even kind of knew he did it, but they couldn't prove it."

"Then how do you know?"

"Because I heard it happen."

"You heard it? Bullshit. Why didn't you wake me up?"

"I was scared. I was in our room. We roomed together in the old house."

"Yeah, I remember."

"Well, that night, before we went to bed, Mom and Dad had a horrible fight. They seemed to make up, but later after Dad had supposedly gone hunting, he came back home."

"How do you know?"

"I heard when he came back. After we were asleep, I heard Mom yelling. I tried to go out to calm them down, but the door was blocked, I couldn't get out."

"Why didn't you wake me?"

"I can't believe you didn't wake up. But I was so scared I didn't know what to do. I didn't want you to be scared too, I guess. Anyway, I tried to get out but I couldn't. There was something blocking the door. At first when they heard me they stopped fighting for a bit, at least I thought they did, but I think they just lowered their voices. I stood by the door listening. I could hear voices first in Mom and Dad's bedroom, then down in the family room, talking and then all of the sudden I heard Mom scream. I screamed then, too, but she didn't hear me. She just screamed."

Again Mike just sat, listening.

"I guess that is when he killed her. I can still hear her screams, Mike. Then all of the sudden they stopped."

Charlie

"What did you do?"

"I stood by the door, listening. After a while I heard steps walking through the kitchen, up to our room. I was right by the door, afraid to move. I heard the steps stop on the other side of the door."

"Holy shit."

"I didn't say anything, didn't even breath. After about a minute, I heard the steps walk back away. For the next hour or so I could hear him walking around. I think trying to hide evidence or something, I don't know."

"How do you know it was Dad?"

It Billy's mind it had to have been him, but for Mike he needed more, so he lied. "Because I heard his voice."

Billy let this all sink in for a while. Mike sat there thinking.

"Why would Dad have killed her?"

Billy stared at him for a minute and then said, "You can't tell any one any of this Mike, ever."

"Okay, okay. Why would he have killed her?"

Billy got up and walked over to his daypack. He opened the sort of hidden pocket in the bottom and pulled out a plastic bag with some papers inside. He carefully took out the papers and handed Mike the note from their mom's lover, the last note.

Mike sat reading it. When he finished he turned it over, looking for a signature.

"What is this? Where did you get it?"

"It's a love letter to Mom. She, well, I guess she was seeing some other man."

"Where did you find it?"

"About a month before Mom died, I saw her hiding a bunch of letters. After she was killed I got them."

"Why didn't you tell the police?"

"Because I didn't want them to arrest Dad."

He pondered that. "But maybe this guy did it?"

"No, this is why Dad killed her. He was so mad that she was cheating that he killed her."

Billy paused for a moment and then said, "I didn't tell you all of this for all these years because I didn't want you to think badly of Mom."

"But she was cheating on Dad."

"Yeah, but he must have driven her to it, Mike. He was so tough, so mean. I think she was just lonely."

"Dad isn't that mean, Billy."

"He has gotten better. He has to be, Mike, he has to cover for this for the rest of his life, so he puts on this nicer act, but you can still see how mean he is underneath sometimes. You know it. You know I'm right."

Mike didn't agree, but he didn't disagree either.

"Why are you telling me all of this?"

"Because we have to stop him."

"Stop him from what?"

"From doing it again."

"From killing someone? Who?"

"Me for one, or maybe even Betsy."

Mike scoffed at him. "You're fucking nuts. He might kill you, but he loves Betsy."

"No, he doesn't. He's nice to her, but he doesn't love her. All these late nights and weekends working, I think he's got a girlfriend now."

"That's such bullshit. He's working late because he's fed up with you."

Billy regretted his last comment and backtracked. "Well maybe not, but he killed Mom and he might just do it again, Mike. Someone's got to do something about it."

"What do you want to do?"

Billy knew he had to be really careful here. "I don't know. I have thought about going to the police, but I don't think this would be enough to prove it."

"Between the letters and you telling them you heard Dad come back, I think, if it is true, that it would be." Mike stopped himself. "This is all bullshit. Dad didn't kill anyone."

"I'm telling you he did, Mike. I heard him. The dogs didn't bark. We have the letters. It was him."

"I don't know, fuck, why are you telling me this?"

"Because I'm scared. I think he's going to kill me. And even if he doesn't, we have to do something. He killed our Mom."

They both sat there for quite a while. Mike read the letter a few more times.

"Do you think we should tell all of this to Betsy?"

"I thought about that, but she wouldn't believe us and if she confronted Dad, I hate to think what he might do to her."

Chapter 43

The next morning they got up early and broke their camp, carefully packing everything away and leaving no trace other than matted grass and a well-watered fire pit. They worked quietly, not discussing the prior night's conversation.

As they were finishing the dogs started to bark excitedly as the rest of their family approached. Jim smiled approvingly at the spotless campsite but was surprised to receive a guarded response, especially from Mike. Immediately, he wondered just what his oldest son had been up to.

Chapter 44

Billy knew that if he wanted to bring Mike into his plan he would have to do it slowly. He knew he shouldn't push.

He wanted to create as much conflict as he could between Mike and his father. And the two were close, so it would be no easy task.

In the weeks after their campfire trip Mike had not mentioned their conversation once. Bill decided that for a while at least, he wouldn't either.

A month or so after he turned eighteen, Bill began the next phase of his plan. One Saturday night, when he was heading out to meet his friends, Bill asked Mike if he could drop him off anywhere. Mike was a little shocked by this because usually Bill just took the old pickup that their parents had gotten for them and left him to fend for himself.

As they pulled out of the driveway Bill asked, "What are you up to tonight?"

"Nothing much. A few of us are meeting at Brian's house."

"Are his parents there? Do you want me to get you some beer?"

"No, they're out and yeah, that would be great."

"No problem. Just don't tell your friends I bought it for you. I don't mind helping you out now that I'm legal, but I don't want to become the source for your whole group."

They drove to the convenience store on Route 131 where no one knew them and Billy bought Mike a twelve pack of Keystone, the cheapest beer they could find.

As he dropped Mike off at Brian's house, he said, "Just be smart Mike. Don't come home drunk or anything."

"Yeah, yeah. I'll be careful. Thanks again."

Bill drove off. He would be Mike's source of beer and booze and just let nature take its course.

And sure enough about two months later his plan worked out. Mike had gathered money from a bunch of his friends and asked Billy to buy him several cases of beer for a big party at a girl friend's house. The girl lived on the outskirts of Harrison in a rural area and her parents were away for the weekend. The girl's twenty-year-old sister was home, but she had plans of her own and let her younger sister have the party, provided she didn't trash the place and cleaned everything up afterwards.

As they drove from the beer store to the party, Bill said, "Look, Mike, this is way more than I should be buying for you. I could be in huge trouble if this comes back to me."

"It won't. Don't worry."

"It might. If anything happens, I don't want to get in trouble just because I helped my little brother."

"You won't. We're not going to get caught out here. There are no nearby neighbors and Peggy's sister is okay with it."

"Yeah, but still. How many of your friends know I have been buying beer for you?"

"Just Brian and Pete. They know to keep it quiet."

"They better. I don't want to get in trouble for helping you."

"You won't. I promise."

"Alright, see you later."

With that Bill left. But about ninety minutes later he drove by again, to see how things had progressed. This time there were about twenty or thirty cars parked near the house and kids everywhere, on the front porch, the front lawn and in inside. Music was blaring and beer cans were everywhere. It was perfect.

He drove out to the strip mall area outside of Harrison along Route 15. He stopped at a McDonalds and killed some time there, and then after about thirty minutes, he got back in his car and drove to a public phone he had found. The payphone was behind a gas station. He could park there and make the call without much chance of anyone seeing him.

He dialed the number.

"Harrison Police Department."

"Yeah, hi. I'd like to report a wild party. There is a bunch of what look like underage kids and a lot of them look pretty drunk to me. I hate to say anything, but I'm afraid they'll be getting in their cars."

"Can I have your name please, sir?"

"No. I don't want to get involved. I'm just trying to potentially save some lives here. You should send a car out to 126 German Flats Road."

"Sir, please can you give . . ."

He hung up and drove home.

Chapter 45

Mike's curfew was 11:00. At about 11:45 the phone rang.
Betsy answered it.
"Mrs. Williams?"
"Yes."
"This is Officer Ryan Sullivan from the Harrison Police Department."
"Oh my God, is Mike okay?"
"Yes, ma'am. Yes. He's fine ma'am. We have him here. You or Mr. Williams should come down and pick him up, ma'am."
"What happened? Why is he there?"
"He was at a party, ma'am. We brought in a bunch of kids for underage drinking."
"Okay, Officer. Thank you. My husband and I will be right there. Thank you."
Jim had been standing beside her as she took the call.
"What happened? Is he alright?"
"Yes. He's fine. He was arrested I guess. He's at the police station. Apparently he and a bunch of other kids were at a party drinking. We have to go pick him up."
"Okay. I'll go. You stay here."
"Are you sure you don't want me to go?"
"No I'll go."
After having witnessed Susan's excessive drinking, Jim had always been very measured in his own drinking and while he was generally not a stickler about setting a lot of rules with his boys, alcohol was his touch point. He knew the boys would drink and that they would probably try pot and maybe even some other drugs too, but he did everything he could to encourage them not to.

Betsy walked him out to his van. "Stay calm, Jim. You know Mike is a good boy. He has messed up here, but it's not the end of the world."

As he was about to get into the car she took his hand and squeezed it. "He's a good boy."

Jim looked at her, seeming to calm a bit. "I know. Don't worry, I'll be calm."

"I'm coming, too."

She yelled back towards the house. "Billy. Billy?"

A moment later, Billy stuck his head out the front door. "What's up?"

"Just stay here. Your Dad and I are going to get Mike. You stay with Andy."

"Do you want me to get him? Where is he? Brian's?"

"No. We'll get him. Just watch Andy."

Jim and Betsy drove to the station. This was Jim's first official interaction with the police since Susan's murder and he was clearly not happy about it. When they pulled up to the normally quiet station, they were surprised to see about a dozen other civilian cars parked outside.

As they walked in the front door, there was a big group of parents, mostly fathers, by the front desk, waiting for their chance to talk with the officer there. Others were sitting at various desks just inside, signing papers or listening to officers explain exactly what had happened and what the next steps were.

After about fifteen minutes, Jim and Betsy were directed to an officer's desk and Mike was brought out to meet them. He looked disheveled and scared, but not at all drunk. When he saw his parents there, he looked even more scared.

As the officer brought him to them, Betsy strategically placed herself between Mike and Jim.

"I'm sorry, I know I messed up."

Betsy cut him off. He stunk of beer. "Let's just talk about this when we get home."

The officer had been through this many times before and quickly saw that the boy's parents appeared to be quite upset. From the look on his father's face, he suspected that the boy had an awful lot of chores and Saturday nights at home ahead of him.

"There's not much more to do here folks. No charges will be brought. In cases of underage drinking we usually just call the parents and have them come pick the kids up, sometimes here and sometimes at the place where the party occurred. Your son wasn't driving, so there are no issues that way."

Charlie

He turned to Mike. "The drinking age in Pennsylvania is eighteen. You're fifteen. You just broke the law. I do not want to see you here again. Do you understand?"

"Yes, sir. I'm sorry, sir."

"Just don't let me see you here again."

Then he turned back to the parents. "Okay. That's it. You can take him home."

Betsy and Jim both responded, "Thank you, Officer."

As they walked out, Mike tried to start to apologize again, but Betsy cut him off in the sharpest tone either Jim or Mike had ever heard from her. "You've said enough for now. We'll talk when we get home."

Jim just nodded and followed them out.

In the privacy of the car, Mike started to apologize again.

Again Betsy cut him off. "I told you, Mike, be quiet! I am so angry at you right now I could explode!" She gathered herself as both men just listened. "Mike, I can't believe you did this. I can tell you one thing right now. I don't know what your father has planned but as far as I'm concerned you won't be going out for at least a month, at least. And there isn't going to be a leaf on a yard for the entire fall, so help me. Now what happened?"

Mike explained that there had been a big party and that the police had come and that yes, he had been drinking. He didn't know where the beer came from. They just all pooled their money and someone else took care of it.

Betsy virtually interrogated him, hardly giving Jim a chance to speak. By the time she had finished everything that needed to be said had been, several times over. Because Betsy so rarely lost her temper, Mike felt little defiance and simply took his medicine.

"Alright, now go upstairs and get to bed. When your father gets up for his walk tomorrow, I'm going to have him get you up and you can start raking. Good night."

The boy stood and started to go upstairs. He looked to each of his parents and said, "I'm sorry, I really am."

Betsy just glared at him. His father actually smiled and patted his back. "It's alright, Mike. Now go to bed."

That night as she lay in bed, Betsy smiled to herself. The tension between Jim and Billy had dissipated, but it was still just beneath the surface. She didn't want him to have to be the heavy with Mike, too. She hoped she hadn't been too hard on the boy, though she had to admit it had been fun to watch his reaction to her anger and Jim's, too.

Billy, on the other hand, was livid. He had counted on his father going nuts on Mike. Betsy had spoiled everything. He had to think of something else to drive a spike between Mike and his father.

Chapter 46

The following February, Mike turned sixteen and got his learner's permit. Like most sixteen year-old boys, he suddenly wanted to go on every errand just so that he could drive. During the week that meant that Betsy was accompanying him everywhere. He was getting the hang of it, but she winced almost every time he drove by a mailbox or telephone pole as he erred too much to the right, to the passenger's side, especially when passing oncoming traffic.

On the weekends, Jim took him out driving and within a few weeks, the boy was becoming a confident, competent driver.

About two months after he got his permit, Jim and Betsy went to a party for her parents for their fiftieth anniversary. Over the years, the tension over her marrying Jim had dissipated, but they still didn't spend much time together. However, after all the time Betsy had spent with the Andersons over the years, Jim wanted her to go to her own parents' fiftieth and while he wasn't looking forward to it himself, he wanted to go with her.

Betsy's parents lived about forty minutes away and they were having the event at a country club that was another twenty minutes further. That meant that unless they left really early, they wouldn't be home until well after midnight.

Bill saw this as a great opportunity. While Mike's grounding had long since ended, his parents still kept a close eye on him and partly as a consequence and partly because he didn't want to upset Betsy so much again, he had been pretty good since the police incident. But not so good that he didn't see his parents' night out as an opportunity. The problem was going to be Andy. One of the two older brothers would have to stay home with him and Mike figured it would probably be him. Bill, however, had other plans.

After Jim and Betsy left, Mike and Bill were sitting watching Penn State lose to Ohio State on TV.

During a break in play Bill said to Mike, "Listen, I'm pretty tired. I think I'll go over to the convenience store and get some junk food, but after that I think I'll just stay home. So I'll watch Andy. You can go out."

"Really?"

"Yeah. Besides, things have been pretty tight around here for you. You deserve a night out. I'll just mess around with Andy."

"Thanks, Bill. That's great."

While Bill watched the end of the game, Mike called a few of his friends, planning his night out. After the game ended, Bill yelled to Mike, "I'm going to go to the store, I'll be back in about twenty minutes. Watch Andy, ok?"

Mike came from upstairs to meet him.

"Yeah absolutely, but you're still coming back right?"

"Yeah, twenty minutes. I'm just getting some junk food for Andy and me."

"Would you mind?"

"What, beer again?"

"Yeah, just one case."

"I don't know, Mike. Last time I was sure I was going to get nailed."

"Yeah, but you didn't. Come on. You know we won't rat you out. Just one case."

He held out his hand, trying to give him fifteen dollars.

Reluctantly, Bill took the money. "Ok, but don't be so stupid this time. If you get in trouble again they'll be so pissed off."

"I won't. I'm just going over to Jane Eastmere's house. There are only going to be about six of us there."

"Alright. Keystone?"

"Yeah, thanks Bill."

About thirty minutes later Bill walked in the front door with potato chips and some soda for him and Andy. Mike met him at the door.

"Didn't you get the beer?"

"Yeah, I left it in the car. I didn't want Andy to see it."

He looked towards the family room where his little brother was sitting. "Good thinking."

"Do you think you could give me a ride over to Jane's?"

"Well I'd have to bring Andy. I don't know. If he sees the beer we're toast. Can't Brian come get you?"

"He's already there."

"Why don't you just take the car?"

Mike just stared at him.

"What, like you've never taken it around the block when no one is home?"

"Yeah, but this is different."

"It's up to you."

Mike thought about it for a minute. He had, in fact, snuck out and driven the car around the block a few times, but taking it out at night was a whole different matter. He was confident behind the wheel, but if he got caught, that would be it. He'd be grounded for months. Still the thought of driving alone and showing up in a car . . . it would blow his friends away.

"I'll do it."

"Don't let me convince you. I'll drive you there if you want."

"No, I'm good."

Bill extended his hand, dangling the keys. "Are you sure?"

"Yeah. What time do you figure Betsy and Dad will get home?"

"I think around one, but if I were you, I'd be home before midnight."

He looked at his watch and thought it over. "That sounds about right."

"Okay, be careful. If you get caught, we'll all be in trouble."

Chapter 47:

Mike's only trouble spot getting there was in his own subdivision. He drove out with a baseball cap pulled down and his hand half over his face so that none of the neighbors would realize that it was him driving. He was pretty sure none had.

Once he got beyond his own street, he felt pretty confident. He approached Jane's driveway cautiously, nervous that one of his friends' parents might be dropping them off. But everything was clear, so he pulled in. Unfortunately, none of his friends saw him drive in. He got out of the truck and reached into the back for the case of beer. Between it and the truck he found a brown paper bag. Inside there was a bottle of Jack Daniels. Bill must have bought it for him. He was being remarkably cool.

Mike went up to the front door holding the case of beer in front of him with the "Jack" and his keys strategically placed on top. He hit the doorbell with his elbow and Jane and Brian answered the door. They both smiled when they saw the beer and then the whiskey, but it was Brian who realized the significance of the keys.

"You didn't?"

Mike just nodded, smiling from ear to ear.

It was all lost on Jane and she asked, "Didn't what?"

"He drove here. Alone."

By this stage about half of their friends had their licenses so Jane assumed that Mike must have just passed his test. "Hey, congratulations."

Brian looked at her. "No you don't get it. He doesn't have his license yet."

Her eyes widened. "You're kidding?"

Mike just smiled, trying to be cool.

And he tried to stay cool and smart for the next few hours. While his friends drank the beer and the Jack Daniels, Mike just had a couple beers. He was a little nervous about driving home and did not want to get wasted.

Chapter 48

Bill and Andy were having a nice night together, watching TV and eating junk. At about 10:00 Bill said, "Come on Andy, let's go to the convenience store and get some ice cream, I could really go for something sweet."

Andy was game so the two headed out in their Dad's van. Bill drove to a store that he knew had a payphone inside, back by the restrooms.

"Andy, stay in the car. I don't want to bump into one of Betsy or Dad's friends out here with you at this time of night. What kind of ice cream do you want?"

"Mint chocolate chip."

"Okay, you want M&M's or anything else?"

"Yeah, thanks. Plain M&M's would be great."

So Bill went inside. He purposely parked in a spot that was blocked off from the back of the store so that Andy wouldn't see him place his calls.

First he called the Harrison Police Department.

"Hi, I'd like to report some kids. They're having a party at 115 Russell Hill Road. They're drinking and making all kinds of noise."

Before the officer could question him further, Bill hung up.

Next he called Jane's house and asked for Mike.

He could hear both the nervousness and the slight buzz in Mike's voice when he answered. "Please don't tell me they're home?"

"No, but I was talking with Andy and I sort of got the impression from what he heard them saying that they might try to cut it a little short. I think there was some sort of present being given to them after the dinner part and there was dancing, so I'm sure they stayed for a while, but if I were you, I'd be home by eleven. There is no way they'll be home before then."

Bill looked at his watch: 10:05.

"Okay. I'll leave in about fifteen or twenty minutes."

"Yeah, just don't cut it too close. Are you okay to drive?"

"Oh yeah, I'm fine."

"Alright, see you in a bit." Bill hung up.

He bought the mint chocolate chip ice cream and M&M's and headed home. There he made a big bowl for himself and for Andy and just waited.

Chapter 49

At 12:10 the phone rang.
"Hello."
"Mr. Williams?"
"No, this is Mr. William's son, Bill. May I help you?"
"Is your mother or father there?"
"No, they're out. May I ask who's calling?"
"Yes this is the Harrison Police Department. When do you expect them home?"
"They should be home any time now." He increased the concern in his voice. "Is something wrong?"
The officer didn't want to tell another kid what was going on, but he also didn't want to leave him or his parents panicked.
"Please tell your parents to call us as soon as they get home. We have your brother Michael here. He is fine, but they need to come and pick him up."
"Yes, sir? What happened? Is he okay?"
"Yes. He's fine. Just have your parents call as soon as they get home."
"Yes, sir. I will."
Now he waited again. He knew he would get in trouble for not stopping Mike when his parents got home and saw that his pickup was gone, but that was fine.
Twenty minutes later he heard them pull up. They had noticed that the truck was gone so were surprised to see Bill open the door as they walked up the stoop.
His father immediately asked, "Where is your truck? Did it break down or something?"
Bill shuffled his feet. "No."
"Well then, where is it?"
"Um, well, Mike has it."

"Mike?" Betsy asked, genuine shock in her voice.

"Where is he?"

"He's alright. The police called. They have him at the station. He is okay. You're supposed to call them."

His father was really angry now, the angriest he had seen him in years. "Why did you let him take the truck? What were you thinking?"

Bill tried to apologize and admitted he was wrong, but of course, there was nothing he could say.

Five minutes later Jim was off the phone and along with Betsy on his way to the station.

This time there was only one other set of parents there. They were getting their daughter. Jim and Betsy recognized the girl, but didn't know her name.

They approached the desk sergeant, who sent them to an officer's desk in the back.

The officer introduced himself and then went in back to get Mike.

When Mike came out he started to apologize but his father raised his hand and motioned it back and forth. Between that and the looks on their faces, Mike just shut up.

The officer slid a third chair in front of his desk and had them all sit down. From behind his desk he opened a manila folder. He read it for a moment and then looked up at Mike.

"I see this is your second time here, son."

"Yes, sir."

The officer turned to his parents. "Well you've been through this before. We picked your son up at the Eastmere's residence on Russell Hill Road. A neighbor reported a party there. Fortunately there weren't any cars involved, so as with the last time, we just call the parents to pick the child up."

Jim and Betsy were both surprised to realize that the police didn't know Mike had driven there and each had the sense not to ask.

The officer saw a momentary look of confusion on the parents' faces, but didn't know what to make of it. He also saw how angry they both looked. Feeling a little sorry for the boy, he said, "For what it's worth, your son seemed to be the only one there who wasn't falling over drunk."

They each nodded, but understandably didn't seem to be at all less angry.

Charlie

The officer turned his attention back to Mike. "Look, Michael, this is twice in about six months that you have been here. You don't want to come back here. Do you understand that?"

"Yes, sir."

"Alright. You're free to go."

Chapter 50

Before Mike could say a word, Betsy cut him off. Once they were inside the car, Betsy's car with Jim driving and Betsy next to him, they both turned to face him. His father spoke this time.

"Did you drive to that party?"

"Yes, sir."

Jim's jaw clenched. He visibly tried to calm himself.

"Where is the truck now?"

"It's at Jane's house."

Betsy asked, "Was she taken in, too?"

"Yes, we all were. There were five of us."

Betsy went on. "Five of you made all of that noise? Enough noise for a neighbor to call the police?"

"We were just watching TV. I don't understand it."

His father, who had not had a drink that night because he was driving and never, ever wanted to give the police a reason to arrest him again, cut him off. "I can smell the beer on you. Don't tell me you were just watching TV."

"No, sir. I didn't mean that. We were drinking, but we were not making any noise."

"Someone heard enough noise to call the police. So you must have been doing something." Betsy seemed as mad as his father. She turned to him.

"Should we go pick up the truck now?"

"Yeah, I guess that make's sense."

Mike reluctantly spoke up. "I don't have the keys. They're in Jane's house." He didn't say that he left them there intentionally so that the police wouldn't notice them on him.

"Betsy, why don't I take you and him home? There is another set there. Bill and I can go get the truck, either tonight or maybe in the morning."

They drove the rest of the way home in silence. As they walked up to the house, Jim said, "You can take your driving test when you turn seventeen. Go to bed."

"Please, I'm sorry, I won't do it again. You can't make me wait another year."

"Go to bed. I don't want to hear another word."

Chapter 51

The next morning Jim and Bill went to pick up the truck. While Bill waited beside it in the driveway Jim knocked on the door and apologized to the Eastmeres for leaving it there, but said he did not want to bother them so late the night before.

Mr. Eastmere sort of took the attitude that most of this was Mike and the other boys' fault, but Jim had the feeling that he especially blamed Mike, because of his "situation." He didn't even ask about the other set of keys. He just quietly took the not-so-subtle abuse from Eastmere and then drove off, slowly and cautiously, following Bill home, repressing his anger.

Chapter 52

Things were very tense around the Williams house for the next few months. The tension between Jim and Bill was palpable. And things with Mike, while not nearly as bad, were also strained.

Betsy and Jim both felt that they should take a hard line with Mike. While they fully understood that teenagers do stupid things, they each felt that they had clearly over coddled Billy and they were not pleased with the results. They didn't want to make the same mistake with Mike. While neither intended to make him wait all the way until his seventeenth birthday to drive again, they did not see any point in telling him that, for a while at least.

To make matters worse still, the atmosphere at Square Box where Jim worked had changed significantly. Griesch had two daughters and neither was interested in the family business. For years a number of larger companies had been interested in Square Box and the prior September, a German manufacturer had made a very aggressive bid for the company at just the right time. The Griesch girls had both graduated from college and moved on. Jeff and Amy were spending more and more time in Florida and New York and less time in Greenville. Jeff was ready to sell and the price was very right.

He tried to do the best he could to ensure the jobs of his employees, but in the end, he had little control over how the new owners would run things once he was gone. And on October 1st, he was gone.

The new management's influence was felt almost immediately. The plant's work atmosphere changed from one in which the employees went from feeling like a part of a team to feeling like insignificant cogs. From Jim's more narrow perspective, his role diminished from a trusted go-to guy to just another employee. Griesch's chief engineer Scott Oats retired with the change of management and his replacement was a German technocrat who didn't think that anyone who wasn't an engineer was worth consulting on anything.

As a result Jim's job and the enjoyment he took from it changed dramatically and for the worse.

For the first time in his life, Jim felt sorry for himself and started to become increasingly sullen.

From Bill's perspective, things were progressing beautifully. He had intended for Mike to get caught driving drunk without a license. The fact that he hadn't been and that only his parents knew that he had been driving without a license ended up working out even better for him, as things often did. Rather than the law punishing Mike, it was only his parents who did. And whenever he got the chance, Bill emphasized to Mike that it was mostly his father who was behind the punishment.

Still, he knew he was going to need to do much more to get his brother to go along with his plan. Somehow, he had to prove to him that his father had killed their mother and that he was capable of doing it again.

Chapter 53

In the months following the second run in with the police, Betsy worked hard to keep her family together. She did eventually tell Mike that if he behaved he wouldn't have to wait until his seventeenth birthday, but that before he would get his license he had to re-earn their trust. He understood and toed the line.

Bill knew he couldn't orchestrate many more incidents and felt that if he was going to get Mike to go along with his plan, he would have to do it soon. The problem was that for his plan to work, Bill needed Mike to be mad at his father and at the same time, needed his father and Betsy to be sufficiently comfortable with Mike to trust him enough to allow him quite a bit of freedom.

During the time since the second incident, Bill had been quiet and helpful with Betsy especially and had encouraged Mike to do the same, largely by example. As a consequence, both boys were re-earning her trust. Between the situation at work and the ongoing, subtle tension with Bill, their father had grown increasingly detached and was less involved in the boys' day-to-day lives than he had ever been. When he was home he was short tempered and sullen. Once again, things were playing into Bill's hands.

One afternoon when he was driving home from school with Mike he had an idea that he thought would finally allow him to implement his plan. In Mike's pile of books he noticed *Walden*.

"How do you like that book? *Walden*?"

Mike looked at him. And rolled his eyes. "Painful."

"No, really, it's not. You just have to read it the right way."

"What are you talking about?"

"Think about how he is living, on his own, off the land. Wouldn't you love to live that way for a while? Not for ever, but for a while?"

Mike thought about it for a minute. "I don't know."

"When I read it, I loved it. In fact, I had this great idea about an independent study project that would tie into it."

This got Mike's interest. He was struggling with what to do for his project. "What was the plan?"

"I wanted to go up to Concord and camp alone for a long weekend. The idea was to just live off the land for a few days, only on what I caught or picked. And for my project I would chronicle the trip, the way Thoreau did."

"Wow, that sounds pretty cool. Why didn't you do it?"

"I asked, but Dad and Betsy wouldn't let me. They said I was too young."

"Well then there's no way they'll let me do it."

Bill let that sit for a while then, as if he had just thought of it, said, "Maybe not, maybe they would let you do it if I went along. Their main objections had been that I was a new driver and that I was too young to be up there alone."

Mike clearly liked the idea, but was skeptical. "It would be great, but after all the shit I've been in, there's no way."

"Maybe if we convince Betsy first."

They discussed it for a while and decided that Mike should to try to sell the idea to Betsy first. They knew that for adventuresome things like this she could be harder to convince than their dad. But Bill knew that it would be easier to convince her this time because she was trying to be the peacekeeper.

She tentatively agreed and that night at dinner brought it up with Jim. Surprisingly, he went along with the plan, Betsy thought out of indifference, which worried her.

Chapter 54

The next day Mike discussed his plan with both his English teacher and the teacher overseeing his independent study. They each thought that it was a great idea.

Mike spent the next few weeks finishing *Walden* and planning the trip. He tried to learn as much as he could about what edible, late fall plant and animal life he might find in northwestern Pennsylvania to survive off of. Bill left it to him, but joked that he wasn't trying to be Thoreau and could hike out to the car and to McDonalds if he got hungry.

Separately, he did his own planning.

Chapter 55

Three weeks later, on the Friday afternoon of the Veteran's Day long-weekend, the boys set off. The night before Jim and Betsy had gone over their plans with them for about the tenth time. They had agreed that the boys should have some food with them in the car, just in case. They would leave it there, but use it in the event they could not catch or find enough to sustain them. They went over safe plants they should be able to find and talked about what fish might still be around and what sort of lures would work best.

Betsy was glad to see Jim drawn into the adventure as she hoped he would be. To Bill's dismay, he was the most enthused he had been in months.

That afternoon, right after school, the boys left.

On the way up, Bill told Mike about his plan.

The boys were scheduled to sleep in the woods on Friday, Saturday and Sunday night. Rather than parking at the Hendries', the boys were going to park on a rural road, about five miles east of there, nearer to a good sized pond where they intended to camp and, more importantly, fish.

"Okay, here's the plan, Mike."

"What plan?"

"We're driving up tonight, but we're coming back early Sunday morning."

"No, we're not. I have to do this project Bill."

"Don't worry, you can still do the project, but we're going to do another project as well."

"What?"

"It's time to do something about Mom's murder, Mike."

"What are you talking about?"

"You know what I'm talking about. I want to scare the hell out of Dad. You've seen how he's been acting lately. I'm afraid he is going to do something horrible again. We have to do something about it. We have to send him a clear message."

"Why? He's upset about work. He'll figure it out."

"No, it's more than that. Way more."

"What are you talking about?"

Bill paused for a minute. He knew he needed to convince Mike, to get him to really believe, so once again, he lied. "Last weekend I went down into the basement to get something and I found Dad down there, at his workbench. We haven't been alone in the same room in a while. When he saw it was me, he just stared at me for a minute, Mike, and then he did something that scared the hell out of me."

"What?"

"He turned his back to me and took something from the drawer of his bench. Then he turned back around to face me." Bill paused as if he was remembering.

"He looked back up at me and staring right at me he held his hammer in his right hand and slowly struck it into his left palm, over and over again."

As Bill drove, he could feel Mike staring at him.

"He was so cold, so sure of himself, Mike. He was telling me he did it and that he'd do it again."

Mike didn't say anything. He just sat there.

Bill was quiet, too. He just let the image fester.

After a while, Mike said, "What do you want to do?"

Originally Bill had intended to bring Mike fully into his plan, but over the past few months, as he thought it over and over, he knew he couldn't. Instead he would make him an unwitting participant and draw him so far in that he would be complicit.

"Like I said, I want to scare him. Really scare him."

He spent the next ninety minutes outlining his scheme.

Early on Sunday morning, when their father was out for his walk, Bill would run him off the road, to scare the shit out of him. So that he didn't recognize the pick-up until the last minute, they would drive the Hendries' Bronco down. Bill had purchased two walkie-talkies and he showed them to Mike.

The plan was that at 4:30 on Sunday morning Bill would drop Mike off about a mile passed and west of the end point of their father's normal walk, on a really windy part of the road. Bill would turn around and drive back past where their street, Dunvegan, intersected with Route 131, the rural road where Jim and the dogs generally walked. About 300 yards east of the intersection, the road was curved. But beyond the curve it was perfectly straight for about a mile.

Bill would park in a wooded area at the end of the straightaway nearest Dunvegan just around the curve. From that point he could see the intersection of Dunvegan and 131 to his west and could see down the straightaway for almost a mile to his east. At the other end, three miles to his west, Mike could watch for traffic coming from the west. At 5 o'clock on a Sunday morning, there wasn't likely to be any.

When Bill saw his Dad and the dogs walk from Dunvegan onto 131, he would wait about eight minutes, until his father was well away from the last house on Dunvegan and on a really desolate part of 131. At that point, he would call Mike on the walkie-talkie. If he got the western all clear from Mike and there was no traffic coming from the east, Bill would speed towards his father. As he approached he would honk a couple of times, to get his attention. Then he would drive at him, going full speed. At the last second he would pull away. His plan was to let his father see him, to know he could have killed him if he wanted.

He would swerve around him and keep going. Then he would pick up Mike and they would drive back to Concord. With luck, no one would see them. Their dad would never know that Mike had been there. When they got home, if his father confronted him, Mike could say Billy left while he was sleeping and showed up the next morning. Mike would be totally safe. Their father wouldn't even tell Betsy. He hadn't told Betsy that Bill accused him of killing their mother and he wouldn't tell her this either, it would just be between the two of them.

Chapter 56

On Sunday at about midnight the boys hiked over to the Hendries'. By 1:30 AM they were in the Hendries' Bronco and on their way to Harrison.

As they drove down Bill was careful to go the speed limit. He didn't want to attract any attention or arrive in Harrison too early. Mike was extremely nervous and Bill needed to manage him, to keep him calm.

At 4:15 he dropped Mike off at the spot he had previously scouted out.

"You stay back in the woods, behind the trees." He point to a spot about twenty feet from the road. "From back there, you can see everything, but no one will see you. Just stay there until I come back. That way, there won't be anyway for Dad to know you were here."

Mike looked scared but he went along.

"Just call me on the walkie-talkie if you get scared Mike, I'll be right here."

By 4:30 Bill was parked in his spot, well off the road and facing towards Dunvegan.

He picked up his walkie-talkie. "Mike?"

After a few seconds the walkie-talkie cackling cleared and he heard Mike's voice. "Yeah?"

"You still awake?"

"Yeah."

"Seen any cars?"

"No, none."

"Okay. Well stay alert and stay hidden. It shouldn't be much longer."

Bill put down his walkie-talkie and took a large gray wool blanket and a roll of twine from inside. Then he reached under the Bronco's steering wheel and popped the hood. He checked down the straightaway for lights. There were none. He got out of the truck and cautiously walked around to the front of the car.

He folded the heavy, coarse wool blanket three times so that it was about four feet long and three feet wide. He squeezed it in his fingers. It was about two or three inches thick. Width-wise, it was about half as wide as the front of the truck. He opened the hood and draped the blanket over the right side of the grill, the driver's side. On top he let one fold hang down into the engine compartment. It was perfect. The bottom hung down below the bumper and half of the front of the truck was covered, padded. He tied the blanket to the front of the truck, dropping twine down into the engine compartment and bringing it up from under the bumper over the blanket, over the grill and back up into the engine opening. He wrapped it around again and again and then tied it off. Then he forced the hood closed, squeezing the single fold between it and the truck's frame, holding the blanket even more firmly in place.

Then he got back in the truck and waited.

Fifteen minutes later, at about 5:05, he saw the first the dogs and then his father walk out onto and across 131. He was carrying a flashlight, but the sun was just below the horizon. Bill felt his heart race.

He waited for about two minutes and then called Mike. "Any traffic?"

"No, none. Have you seen Dad yet?"

"Yeah, he's on 131. Let's wait five more minutes."

"Bill, this a really bad idea. Let's not do it."

"I'm just going to scare him."

"No, I'm out."

"Fine you're out. Then I'm still going to do it, but I'm not going to pick you up. Dad will know you're down here."

"Come on. No. Don't do it."

"I'm just going to scare him, Mike. If he doesn't get the message, if he is still all freaky after this, I'll go to the police with everything."

Mike was quiet on the other end.

"I'm going to call you back in about three minutes. Give me the all clear. If you don't, I'm going anyways and I'm leaving you."

"Fuck."

Bill signed off.

For two more minutes he waited. His father and the dogs were around a bend out of his sight. There was no traffic behind him. He looked at his watch. 5:13. He made himself wait one more minute.

Charlie

He looked over his shoulder again. There were still no cars behind him.

At 5:14 he picked up the walkie-talkie. "All clear?"

No response.

"All clear?"

The static cleared. "It's clear. Don't get too close. Just scare him."

Bill dropped the transmitter onto the seat behind him and looked into the rearview mirror. Seeing nothing, he pulled out onto 131 with his headlights still off and tentatively moved forward. His heart was racing as he slowly drove along. He passed Dunvegan and then slowed as he approached the curve.

As he circled the curve he saw his father's back in the distance. The dogs were about twenty feet ahead of him, unleashed.

Still moving slowly Bill touched on the gas several times, revving the engine. He thought he could see his father turning to look over his shoulder. He revved again. His father stopped and turned around. Bill accelerated and then turned on the headlights.

His father's hand went up, shielding his eyes. He was about 100 yards away now. Bill had to decide. Part of him didn't want to, couldn't. He slowed and at about 50 yards, stopped altogether. He could see him trying to make out the car, trying to understand. He took his foot of the brake and gunned the engine. For a moment his father was frozen, still. Bill tried to see a sign of recognition on his face, but there was none.

He was bearing down on him now, yards away. Still his father's face showed no recognition, only fear. He started to run for the side of the road but he was too late. Bill swerved left to try to catch him with the blanketed part of the front of the car.

He was on him. His face was turned away. The look of recognition, of guilt that Bill had pictured so many times was not there. There was only his back and then an impact, loud and solid. His father went from his view. He felt his tires pass over him. The front tires, and then the back.

Bill maintained control and swerved back out onto 131 from the brim. He slowed but didn't stop. The dogs were barking frantically. He looked in the rear view mirror. The brim wasn't in his line of sight. He looked over his shoulder, trying to focus, searching. His eyes caught the movement of the dogs and then his body. It appeared still.

He accelerated and went around the curve.

Three minutes later as he was still about a half a mile from where he had left Mike, he saw a figure running towards him. It was Mike.

Bill pulled up beside him. Mike saw the blanket on the front of the car.

"What did you do?"

"Hurry up, get in."

"What?"

"Get in. Now."

Bill put the truck in park and got out, grabbing Mike by the coat. He pushed him into the back seat. Then he slammed the door on him and got back in.

"Fuck, Bill, what did you do?"

Bill didn't say anything. He just drove. He had to get off of 131. In another mile he turned north. Still he hadn't passed a car. After another five minutes he pulled off to the side and popped the hood. Using his knife he cut away the twine and pulled off the blanket. He stuffed it into a garbage bag and threw it into the back of the truck.

Mike just sat in the back seat, with his head in his hands.

Twenty minutes later they were on the interstate, heading back to Concord.

Chapter 57

At 6:37 Betsy heard her doorbell ring, or at least she thought she did. It rang again. She realized it must have been ringing for a while, because it had become part of the dream she was having. She looked at her clock and then for Jim. He must still be out walking.

She stood up and looked out her front window. There was a police car.

Without even grabbing a robe, she ran down the stairs and opened the front door. The police chief, Matt Mason, was standing there.

"What is it? What's happened?"

Mason looked afraid. "Mrs. Williams, there's been an accident. It's your husband."

From the look on his face she knew the answer before she asked. "Is he?"

The chief nodded.

Betsy didn't react. She just stood, lost. Mason tried to give her a minute but nothing changed. She stood still, in her doorway, in her nightgown. Finally Mason stepped forward, into her house. Standing beside her, he put his left hand on the top of her right shoulder and put his right arm around her upper back. He looked around and then led her into the living room, onto a couch. Carefully he sat her down and wrapped her in a throw blanket that had been draped over the back of the couch.

He knelt upright in front of her, his eyes almost level with hers. Hers were blank.

"Mrs. Williams?"

He touched her shoulder. "Mrs. Williams?"

Her eyes came into focus. She looked at him.

"What happened?"

"There was an accident. He was hit by a car."

"An accident?"

Mason saw doubt in her eyes.

"Yes, well, we think so. A hit and run."

"Where is he?"

"He's in an ambulance."

With the word ambulance her eyes showed hope and again Mason had to confirm his death, turning his head from side to side, with the smallest turns he thought would still convey his message.

"What was he doing out there at this time of day, Mrs. Williams?"

"He was walking the dogs. He does it every morning. Where are the dogs?"

"They're in my truck, ma'am."

"Where are they taking Jim?"

"To the hospital Ma'am." Then to again discourage any false hope he added, "To the morgue there, Mrs. Williams."

"I want to see him. Can you take me to him?"

"Yes, ma'am. Why don't you go get dressed and then I'll take you to him?"

Chapter 58

At about 7:15 she came back downstairs.

"Our son Andrew is upstairs asleep. What should I do? Should I wake him?" Even as she asked she started to cry again. How could she tell him that his father had died? How could she tell Bill and Mike? First their mother and now this?"

Mason thought for a moment. Andrew was the youngest. The last time he had seen him he had been an infant.

"I think we should probably wake him, ma'am. How old is he now?"

"He's nine, almost ten. He worships Jim."

"Do you want me to wake him?"

She thought for a minute, not about whether to let Mason tell him, but rather about what she would say. "No, I will."

"Where are the other boys, ma'am? Billy and Mike?"

Betsy was surprised that he knew their names, but realized from his use of Billy rather than Bill that he had known them from years earlier.

"They're away for the weekend."

Before he could follow up she wearily went up the steps.

Mason went out to his car and got the dogs. When he had arrived on the scene, the dogs were barking wildly. They were different dogs than the ones Mason had known, but the chief suspected he could control them. As he had so many years before, he had the other officer on the scene, Tim Wright, step back. Then he calmed the dogs by whispering, "Charlie."

Now he took the dogs from his truck and let them loose in their yard. They sat outside the kitchen door, waiting for their breakfast.

Twenty-five minutes later Betsy and Andy came down the steps.

Chapter 59

A little while after that Bill and Mike parked the Bronco at the Hendries' and put the keys back inside their cabin.

Bill wiped down the inside of the truck and then checked out its front. The truck did have a dent in the left front, but it was hardly distinguishable from the many, many others on the battered old Bronco.

He grabbed the garbage bag with the blanket from the truck and the fishing gear they had left at the cabin the night before and headed out. His plan was to go to a good fishing spot he knew that was a long way from both their campsite and the Hendries'. Mike was despondent. He just followed Bill, saying nothing.

An hour later they reached the spot. Bill wrapped the blanket around some rocks and tied them in it and threw it into a deep part of the lake. Then he joined his brother and sat, fishing and waiting. Bill caught two small mouth bass.

Chapter 60

On the way to the hospital Chief Mason was finally able to ask where the two older boys were.

"They're away camping, up near Concord."

Mason couldn't believe what he had just heard. His mind raced. He didn't want to panic the boys' stepmother, but he wanted to find them as quickly as possible.

"Mrs. Williams, I think we should find the boys right away, so that they can get down here to be with you. I'm going to call in their location to my office and have the police up in Concord find them for us." Again to reassure her he added. "They should be here with you, ma'am."

Andy helped the chief narrow down where to find the boys and he called it into his office. The Concord police knew the area Andy described and almost immediately found the boys' truck. Its engine was cold.

Forty-five minutes later they found their campsite. The boys weren't there.

It wasn't until noon that they did find them, fishing on a pond about an hour's hike north of the campsite.

Three and a half hours later, the state troopers delivered Bill and Mike to their home. The boys were surprised to see many of their neighbors gathered around police cars that cut off their driveway from the rest of the street. As the troopers' car slowly pulled through the parted crowd, Bill could see the sympathetic looks on their faces. Those were looks he had anticipated.

Two Harrison police vehicles were parked on their driveway, a truck that belonged to the chief and a patrol car. The chief and two other officers were standing in the driveway.

When the boys stepped from the troopers' car, Chief Mason approached them.

By now Mason knew that there was no accident. There were skid marks on the road. The marks showed that the driver had apparently peeled out fifty-some yards in front of where Williams' body had been found. The skid marks ended and then a trail of tire tracks appeared on the dirt and gravel brim. The tracks swerved to where the corpse was first hit, but did not seem to show any indication of having slowed. They continued beyond the body and then turned back out onto the paved road.

Whoever did this had stopped and then apparently intentionally run him over.

From talking with Mrs. Williams, Mason now knew that Williams had left his house at 5. He must have been killed at about 5:15. The boys were found at noon. They could have easily driven up to Concord. It was just like before. With all of his heart he hoped he was wrong.

Mason looked them over as they approached. They weren't the little boys he had met all those years ago.

He extended his right hand to Bill and then to Mike. Each one shook his hand firmly. Bill looked him straight in the eye. Mike couldn't. Just by looking at him, Mason knew.

He looked to the state trooper and the trooper nodded.

Sympathetically, he asked, "You've been told about your father?"

They both nodded.

Inside the dogs were barking frantically. The kitchen door opened and Betsy and Andy came out. She took both boys in her arms and hugged them tightly, crying and kissing them.

The three dogs pushed out through the partially opened kitchen door and ran wildly, barking and circling the officers and the Williams.

Mason watched as the family ignored them, just trying to console each other. Only Billy seemed to be in control.

The dogs kept barking and barking, running wildly around the group, somehow sensing the anguish of their owners.

The younger officer tried to quiet the dogs, but they just kept barking. The family seemed oblivious. They just stood there, hugging and crying and talking. The dogs kept barking and barking, running in circles around the Williams, jumping at them, barking and yelping.

Betsy tried to explain what had happened and the dogs barked, over and over again.

Finally the other officer, Officer Toyne couldn't take the barking anymore. He turned to them and yelled, "Charlie."

Mason and Billy turned to face Toyne. Simultaneously all three realized their mistakes.